This book must be returned by the date specified at the time of issue as
the DATE DUE FOR RETURN.
The loan may be extended (personally, by post, telephone or online) for
a further period if the book is not required by another reader, by quoting
the above number / author / title.

Enquiries: 01709 336774

www.rotherham.gov.uk/libraries

Annie repeated the words the instant they left her lips. How was it that she felt so self-conscious?

Maybe because of that dream you had about him last night?

"Are you all right?" Trace asked.

"Hmm?" She innocently shifted her gaze to his handsome face.

Silence fell between them and Annie did her best to focus solely on her girls, but it wasn't easy when she was so aware of the guy leaning on the fence a few feet away. And it was even more difficult when he said, "Would you like to go riding sometime?"

"Is that an invitation?"

"It is."

"Because you're looking for company?"

"Partly."

"The other part?"

His gaze traveled over her in a way that warmed her. "Because I wouldn't mind going riding with you."

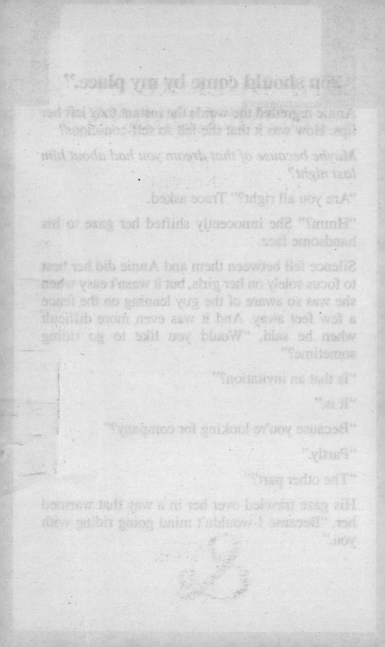

THE BULL RIDER'S HOMECOMING

BY
JEANNIE WATT

First Published in Great Britain 2016
By Mills & Boon, an imprint of HarperCollins*Publishers*
1 London Bridge Street, London, SE1 9GF

© 2016 Jeannie Steinman

ISBN: 978-0-263-92021-5

23-0916

Our policy is to use papers that are natural, renewable and recyclable products and made from wood grown in sustainable forests. The logging and manufacturing processes conform to the legal environmental regulations of the country of origin.

Printed and bound in Spain
by CPI, Barcelona

Jeannie Watt lives in a historic Nevada ranching community with her husband, horses, ponies, dogs and cat, Floyd. When she's not writing, Jeannie loves to horseback ride, sew vintage fashions and, of course, read romance.

To Bill Swanson—
this bull-riding romance is for you!

Chapter One

"Mom!"

"Just a sec, honey…" Annie Owen squinted at her sewing machine, trying to turn a tight corner. Just a few more stitches and—

"Mom!"

Annie jumped from her chair, recognizing the something's-about-to-explode tone in her daughter's voice just as she heard the awesome sound of water spraying against…something. She raced into the kitchen, skidding to a stop to gape at the stream of water shooting wildly out of the tiny utility room and hitting the hallway wall.

"Get back," she automatically ordered her seven-year-old twin daughters, who were inching closer to the utility room, green eyes wide. Picking up a towel from the laundry basket and using it as a shield, she approached the wild hose that had broken free from its clamp during the rinse cycle and was now shooting water in all directions. She made a grab at it just as the doorbell rang.

"Peek through the side window and see who that

is," she called as she made another grab at the hose. She caught it but now that she had the spewing hose, what was she going to do with it? She had to turn the water off somehow and she couldn't reach the faucet behind the washer.

"Stranger," Katie called. "A guy."

Great.

Annie opened the washer lid and tried to jam the hose inside but it instantly came free, banging the lid open and spraying her full on, soaking her hair. Sputtering, she wiped her hands over her face and slicked back her hair.

"He looks like a cowboy," Katie said. "He has a black hat just like Uncle Grady's."

Great. Mystery cowboy.

"Give me a second." Something she was saying way too often of late. Since taking the job at a local Western boutique and putting in all the hours she possibly could, she seemed to be one step behind the action, playing catch-up. But she loved her job. Truly she did. Finally she was gaining financial ground, and that felt great.

She wiped her face on the wet towel then tried to turn off the faucet, but it refused to budge. Finally she wrapped the towel around the hose, which stopped the spraying but not the flow. Muttering a word that the girls weren't allowed to hear, much less say, she made her way out into the living room, marched to the door and opened it as far as the chain would allow. The guy standing on her porch, wearing a hat that really did look exactly like her brother's, was tall, dark and unsmiling. In fact, he looked as if he wanted to be any-

where but where he was. The feeling was mutual. She
wanted him somewhere else, too.

"Can I help you?" she asked with more of a clip in
her voice than she intended.

"Uh," the guy said, looking over her head at the
waterworks going on behind her. The towel had come
loose. "Maybe I can help you."

And let a man she didn't know into the house? She
thought not. "I've got it," she said dismissively.

"I don't think so."

Annie jerked her chin up. "Do you need directions?"
She was about to close the door in his face so she could
deal with her flood.

"I'm Trace Delaney."

Annie blinked at him through the cracked door. She
knew the name from the bull-riding circuit, but had
no idea why the guy would be standing on her porch.
"Grady's on the road."

His frown deepened. "I know. I'm watching Grady's
place for him. Or I guess it's really his girlfriend's
place. He asked me to stop by and check in with you
after I got here." Once again he looked past her at the
water. "Where's the water main?"

"Cellar. I can get it." She didn't like his take-charge
tone, and as far as she knew, Cliff Fife was watching
Lex's place, as he always did when the couple traveled
together. Her brother was very good about keeping her
apprised as to what was going on in his life, and he
hadn't said one word about a change of plans. Or about
a fellow bull rider "checking in" with her.

"You sure?" Trace pointed his chin at the water behind her. Annie wanted to look but didn't.

"Positive." He was most likely Grady's friend as he said, but until she knew what was going on, the guy wasn't coming into the house. Besides the stranger-danger factor, there was something about him that made her feel slightly off center. It was a discomforting feeling. "I'm used to handling this kind of stuff alone and I really need to get at it. Maybe we can talk some other time." She gave him a tight smile and stepped back, getting ready to close the door.

The man opened his mouth as if to argue then seemed to change his mind. He gave a cool nod and turned to head down the porch steps toward a black Ford truck. Annie shut the door and twisted the dead bolt before he'd hit the last step and raced toward the cellar. She could debate her level of rudeness later, after the water was turned off.

"Let me know when he drives away," she called to the girls. "Do not open the door."

"He's driving away," Kristen called as Annie started down the cellar steps.

Excellent. A few minutes later she trudged back up the stairs, thinking that she needed to keep a wrench next to the main. That faucet was hard to turn. And the one behind the washer—that one needed a blowtorch.

Now the aftermath.

"There's a lot of water." Kristen edged up to stand beside her while Katie walked barefoot back and forth through the puddle in the hall.

"Lot of water," Annie agreed, propping her hands

on her hips. She tried hard to face all disaster with equanimity. The girls needed to see that panic helped nothing.

"Why didn't you let the man help?" Katie asked midsplash.

"Because I don't know him." She didn't even know if he was really Trace Delaney, although she couldn't think of one reason why a guy would pretend to be a bull-riding friend of her brother. She'd have to do a Google search as soon as she got her house dried out. She rarely watched bull riding, preferring to get her stress in other ways, so she hadn't a clue as to what Trace Delaney looked like.

"He's Uncle Grady's friend."

"That's what he says, but how do we know for sure?" Annie dropped the towel she still held on the encroaching water, stopping the flow into the kitchen. Lately the teaching moments seemed to be happening with alarming regularity.

"Oh," Kristen said. "He might have been trying to fool us."

"Yes, that's true."

She tried to be matter-of-fact. She didn't want her daughters to grow up frightened—merely sensible. Kristen was a little too fearless; Katie a bit overly cautious. She'd love to edge them both toward a happy medium.

"Girls, why don't you get the bathroom towels? I think this is beyond mopping."

When she was done sopping up water, she was going to call her brother and find out why he hadn't told her someone other than Cliff was watching Lex's place and why that someone was checking in with her. It might all be very innocent, but she was getting a bad feeling… like maybe Grady was trying to fix her up, or, at the very least, getting her a watchdog. She did not need a fix-up and she certainly didn't need a watchdog. She understood that her brother was trying to make up for the time he wasn't there for her as he built his career, but what *he* didn't understand was that she had been fine handling her life on her own then, and she was fine handling it alone now.

SO MUCH FOR DUTY.

Trace hadn't been wild about checking in with Grady's sister from the beginning, but he'd agreed to do so because Grady had been nice enough to offer him a place to stay while he recovered from the shoulder surgery that had put his career on hiatus. Emphasis on *hiatus*. His career wasn't anywhere near over.

But why Grady thought his sister needed looking in on was beyond him. If she handled the waterworks with the same cool efficiency with which she'd handled him, she was probably already mopping up the damage.

If she wasn't…well, he had offered to help.

He slowed as he approached a fork in the gravel road and checked the GPS. Left. He'd never been to this part of Montana, but within a matter of minutes, the GPS successfully guided him to Grady and Lex's small ranch. The property was located almost five miles from that of Grady's sister, so there wasn't much of a chance of him accidentally encountering her while he was running or riding.

As he pulled into the driveway, he half wondered if that was a good or bad thing. No, he hadn't wanted to check in with her, but now that he'd seen her, he had to admit to being somewhat intrigued. The steely glint in her eye as she'd quickly assessed his unworthiness had contrasted sharply with her small, almost delicate stature, her full mouth, the soft blue of her eyes. The front of her light brown hair had been soaking wet and slicked back from her forehead, accentuating the angles of her face, but when she turned to check on her girls, the hair that swung to the middle of her back looked as if it would feel like silk.

He let out a soft snort. If he ever tried to touch her hair, to see if it really did feel like silk, he'd probably find himself on the wrong end of a judo hold or something. Grady might be concerned about his sister, but Trace's first instinct was that, small as she was, she could take care of herself.

Three dogs jumped at the fence when he parked his truck next to a classic GMC pickup. Lex had written their names down and he'd have to match them up to their descriptions as soon as he did a quick check of the other livestock. There was a pen of ducks and several horses grazing in the pasture. All the troughs were filled and the ducks seemed to have plenty of food.

When he returned to the truck and pulled his duffel out of the backseat, a white-and-black cat sauntered out from behind a tree and approached, getting close but not too close.

Felicity. He remembered that name. He'd once dated a Felicity. It hadn't ended well. Hopefully he and the cat would get along better. The cat probably wasn't going to demand that he find a new occupation.

The dogs greeted him with a mixture of suspicion and joy. *Yay, someone is here to feed us! But...who is this guy?*

Whoever he is, I hope he feeds us!

"I'm your new roommate," Trace murmured as he headed up the walk with the entourage of sniffing pooches and one mildly interested feline. He unlocked the door and opened it. To his surprise, the dogs didn't rush in. Instead they plunked their butts down on the porch and stared at him. Lex ran a tight ship.

"All right, you can go in," he said, gesturing toward the inside of the house. He probably didn't have the right command, but the dogs seemed to have understood. They raced past him into the living room and then he waited as the cat took a few slow steps forward then trotted daintily past him.

A neighbor by the name of Cliff had taken care of the place for the past two weeks, and all the animals had been fed for the day. Lex had written detailed feeding instructions and drawn small maps showing him where everything he would need was located. She'd offered him the master bedroom, but after taking a quick tour of the shipshape house, he decided to sleep in the extra room, which, judging from the horse show ribbons on the wall and the collection of rodeo buckles lined up on the bookshelf, had been Lex's childhood room. He dropped his duffel and sat on the bed to take off his boots. Long, long day; long, long drive.

He rubbed his sore shoulder, squeezing slightly to test the depth of the pain, and winced. For once he was going to follow doctor's orders and take it easy for at least another week. An ornery brockle-face bull named Brick was waiting to test him at Man vs. Bull in December, and he was determined to come out on top. Three times he'd tried to ride Brick and three times he'd failed. Not only did he want the purse, which would make up for all the events he was missing while he healed, he also wanted vindication.

To do that he'd have to allow himself to heal fully. He just hoped his head didn't explode from frustration before that happened.

It took most of the evening to chase Grady down. Both his and Lex's phones kept going to voice mail, and Annie began to wonder if he was in an emergency room somewhere. Bull riders tended to spend inordinate amounts of time being checked out by medical personnel, so she was starting to get truly concerned when on the sixth call he answered the phone. "Annie. Is everything all right?"

"I was about to ask you the same. Why didn't you guys answer?"

"No cell service in Calico Valley. We just now drove into range. You called…five times? What's up?"

"Who's watching your place?"

"Trace Delaney is taking over for Cliff. I take it he stopped by?"

"He did. Why didn't you warn me? He came at a rather inconvenient moment and I wasn't all that cordial."

"I'm sorry, Annie." Grady did indeed sound sorry. She could almost see him slapping his forehead. "We threw this deal together at the last minute and then I had a bad ride at Livermore. After that I drove like the wind to make it to Calico…sorry."

"Are you okay?"

"I was in the money last night."

"Congratulations." Annie checked to see if the girls were indeed at the kitchen table working on their reading homework before she said in a low voice, "So why did Trace Delaney check in with me? As opposed to you simply calling me to let me know that you'd changed caretakers?"

"You're my sister," Grady said patiently. "I just thought it would be good if he had a contact while he was there. So I told him how to find your place."

"As opposed to simply giving him my phone number."

"I did that, too."

"You aren't trying to hook us up, right?"

Grady sputtered. "I learned my lesson when I tried to fix you up with Bill Crenshaw in high school."

Not quite true. He'd sent a couple of carefully vetted bull-riding buddies her way over the past couple years, but Annie wasn't in the market for a man—especially a bull rider. Too much stress involved and, besides that, she had her hands full with her girls. Who had time for a guy?

"I hate being blindsided," she finally said.

"I get that and I'm sorry."

"Yeah. Okay…well, ride hard tomorrow."

"Day after."

Annie smiled a little. "The girls send hugs."

"Hugs back," Grady said.

Annie ended the call and settled back in her chair. What was done was done, so why was it bothering her? Because the guy had stopped by at Grady's urging and she'd run him off the property. Not a very nice thing to do.

She needed to explain. Make amends. And maybe get another look at the guy. He'd had kind of amazing hazel eyes, and while she may not be in the market for a guy, there was no reason she couldn't look.

TRACE'S BIGGEST ADJUSTMENT after having the surgery to repair the torn ligaments in his shoulder had been adapting to downtime. Never in his life had he held still for so long. Even busted and cracked ribs hadn't kept him from practicing. A good, tight wrap and he'd been ready to go, but the doctor had been quite clear that if Trace didn't allow himself sufficient healing time with this injury, then he was looking at destroying the work the surgeon had done and perhaps putting himself out of competition forever.

Not going to happen, which meant following orders.

Which also meant champing at the bit as he marked time, watched bull-riding technique videos and exercised the parts of his body that he could. He was eating carefully—lots of protein, not much sugar or bread—

trying to keep the weight off and the muscle intact as he worked his lower body. Legs were important and he wasn't going to lose the strength in his.

When Trace had agreed to watch Grady's place, he'd figured he could spend the hours when he wasn't concentrating on rehab puttering around the place, doing whatever he was capable of with a bum shoulder. Unfortunately, the ranch was in pristine condition and there were no handyman jobs to do. His only duties were to feed the animals twice a day, water Lex's plants and mow the yard. If ever there was an incentive to heal up and get back on the road, this was it.

Grady had called the night before to apologize for the mix-up with his sister. He'd neglected to tell her that Trace would be checking in, so naturally she'd been startled when he'd shown up at her door, acting as if she should be expecting his arrival. And it wasn't as if he'd come at the best of times. The highlight of the call had been when Lex had taken over the phone and asked if Trace would mind exercising her horses. He had a feeling she knew just how much time he'd have on his hands, and the thought of riding off into the not-too-distant mountains appealed. He could ride bareback, work on his balance and leg strength.

First thing Sunday morning Trace experienced the thrill of trying to mount a sixteen-hand mare bareback without jarring his left shoulder. It was doable… kind of. At least there was no one around to see him climb up onto a fence and ease himself onto the horse's back, just like little kids had to do—although it wasn't unlike mounting in the chute. Yeah. That was it. No shame there.

After settling on the mare's back and doing a few practice circles in the wide driveway to make certain that she and he were communicating properly, he started down the road toward the mountains. The dogs complained bitterly about being left behind, but he wasn't going to risk taking Lex's dogs out on the road, no matter how lightly traveled it appeared to be. Riding felt good—no, it felt great—after weeks of being cooped up, and after a good two hours exploring the foothills, he finally headed back, hungry and thirsty. He hadn't expected to explore for so long, but there was no reason for him to hurry back to the lonely ranch.

The ranch, however, wasn't as lonely as he'd left it. He spotted a small white car parked in front of the house when he rode into the driveway and immediately recognized the little girls poking their fingers through the fence at the dogs, who were wiggling ecstatically. Grady's sister and nieces had come to call. Annie was on the way back to her car from the front door when she shaded her eyes against the sun and spotted him.

"Hey!" one of the girls yelled as he rode closer. "That's *my* horse!"

"Katie," her mother warned, and although the girl's mouth clamped shut, she didn't look happy. Trace dismounted stiffly several yards away, sliding down the horse's side carefully, so as not to jar his stiff shoulder too badly, then led the mare up to the car where the girls started petting her shoulder and neck.

"Can I please have Daphne's reins?" one of the girls

asked. Trace looked at Grady's sister. She gave a small nod and he handed the reins over.

"We'll get her a drink," the other twin announced.

Trace watched them lead the mare toward the trough then turned back to find Annie regarding him. Yesterday, with wet hair slicked back from her forehead, she'd been all serious blue eyes and unsmiling lips. Today the long brown hair spilling in waves around her shoulders softened the angles of her heart-shaped face and accentuated the fullness of her mouth, the soft blue of her eyes—but her expression was just as serious as it had been while dealing with a flood and a stranger at the door. Somehow those full lips of hers didn't look right pressed into a flat line.

"Look, I'm sorry for being short with you when you came by the house. I didn't know—"

"It's all right." The naturally husky notes of her voice strummed along his nerves in a pleasant sort of way.

"I was rude."

"Understandable, given the circumstances."

Annie didn't reply. She shifted her weight and looked past him to where her girls were watering the mare, presenting him with her delicate profile. Trace rarely had a problem filling in gaps in conversation, but as she brought her gaze back to his, he found himself at a loss. She was a small thing, serious, yet sexy in a girl next door sort of way…and being near her stirred something deep inside of him. Something he didn't particularly want stirred.

"I appreciate your understanding," she said coolly.

"Not a problem."

No problem at all, although he couldn't help but wonder if being attracted to Grady Owen's sister might introduce a complication or two into his life.

Chapter Two

Trace Delaney was tall for a bull rider. And since Annie was short, she had to look up at him. The guy had great cheekbones, a really nice mouth and, unlike her brother, no visible scars. Deep hazel eyes, more green than brown, studied her solemnly from beneath slightly frowning dark eyebrows, and she realized that she was staring. She pulled her gaze away and a few awkward beats of silence passed. Neither of them seemed able to come up with anything to say, but she refused to shift uncomfortably.

"By the way," she said, breaking the silence. "I'm Annie Owen. Those are my daughters. Kristen in red and Katie in blue."

"Cute kids." At least he didn't say they took after her, as many people did, because they didn't. They looked like their blond-haired, green-eyed father who was long gone. Not that that bothered Annie anymore. She was grateful to be raising her girls alone.

"Thank you." She dove into the reason she'd come. "Obviously there was a miscommunication between

Grady and me, and I wanted to stop by to apologize for chasing you off my porch."

Trace smiled and Annie fought to keep from catching her breath. Holy cow.

"He and I talked. It's fine. Did everything turn out all right last night?"

"After a lot of mopping."

"What about repairs? Do you have someone handling those?"

She looked at him in surprise. "I went to the hardware store for a hose and a new wrench." Because she couldn't find hers and had a feeling it had been involved in some project the twins had cooked up. "We're on our way home now."

"Ah." Again the silence settled in and Annie was about to do them both a favor and call the girls so that they could leave, when Katie and Kristen headed back toward them from the trough, pulling the ever-patient mare behind them.

"She drank a lot," Katie announced, still holding tightly to the reins.

"Warm morning," Trace agreed. "And we went a long way."

Bareback. Annie couldn't help but wonder if his butt was sore. Hers would be. How long had it been since she'd ridden?

Katie tilted her head up. "Can I come and ride Daphne next weekend?"

"Katie!" Annie flashed Trace a quick glance of apology, catching the deer-in-headlights look that crossed his face. He might have been willing to check in with her, but it was blatantly obvious that he didn't want his space invaded. Fine, because she didn't want to invade it. Not when he made her feel so crazy aware of him. Like riding, when was the last time *that* had happened to her?

"We'll wait until Lex comes home to ride," Annie said in her mom voice.

Katie drew in a breath, as if to argue, but Annie cocked an eyebrow and she let out the breath in a whoosh. "All right," she mumbled. She and Kristen turned as one and headed for the car.

"Sorry about that," Annie said.

Trace gave her a tight smile in return. "It probably would be best if they waited for Lex."

Annie gave a nod, even though a small, contrary part of her wanted to say, *Hey, it isn't like you have to be around while they ride.*

"Agreed." The car door opened and closed behind her. "I need to go. Lots of chores ahead of me. Give a shout if you need anything."

He wouldn't. She knew that as certainly as she knew that she was going to spend the drive home explaining why the twins had to wait for Lex to get home before riding the horses they'd ridden regularly for the past several months.

Because that was the way it was. End of story.

WELL, THAT HAD been awkward.

He shook his head as Annie turned her car onto the county road, and then led the mare toward the pasture. Faking small talk was usually easy, but facing off with Annie had triggered the discomfort he'd once felt around people he didn't know. A discomfort he'd worked a long time to overcome.

He'd grown up shy and his mom had been something of a recluse until she passed away just after he'd turned fourteen. They'd moved from apartment to apartment, trailer house to trailer house, looking for ever-lower rent as the medical bills stacked up. They'd stayed in the Reno-Carson City area, but he'd changed schools every year or two and found it was easier to simply keep to himself. That way people didn't ask questions, expect to be invited over. Things like that.

When cancer had finally claimed his mom, he'd been sent to live with his father, who hadn't wanted him in the first place. The last thing he'd wanted was the son who was a reminder of his brief relationship with a Reno cocktail waitress. He'd given Trace food and shelter, but his discomfort with the situation had been palpable, and Trace had found himself feeling even more alone than he had when he'd been in Reno. At least there he'd had his mom and a few acquaintances. That first summer in Oregon, he'd had no one—or at least he hadn't until Ernest McClure had found him exploring on his property and had insisted that he come home and eat lunch with him and his wife, Josie, so that they could get to know "the new neighbor."

Trace had gone, more because he'd been caught trespassing than because he wanted to get to know anyone. Going with Ernest, however, had been the best accidental move of his life. In Ernest and Josie, he'd found pseudograndparents. Mentors. People who believed in his basic good—something he'd kind of wondered about.

Thanks to their gentle influence—which later he discovered was more like velvet-covered steel—Trace started actively working to make something of himself, his life. He'd joined the school rodeo team, and made an effort to connect with other kids. It'd been painful at first, but as he made more friends, he gained confidence, and by the time he'd graduated, he'd learned to play the social game well. He may never have connected with his dad, but he'd done all right. And now he could effect easy conversation with the best of them... except with Annie Owen.

He had no idea what was going on there.

Trace gave a small snort as he closed the tack-room door and pushed the past out of his head. He didn't need to worry about Annie or connecting because he probably wasn't going to see her again. The future was his biggest concern.

The future and the long day on the ranch that stretched out before him.

EVEN THOUGH ANNIE had worked at Annie Get Your Gun for over a year, she still felt like smiling when she walked through the door to start her day. It was a total accident that she shared a name with the store, but she liked being partnered up with Annie Oakley, who was the true namesake.

There was something about the upscale yet funky Western boutique housed on the ground floor of a historic brick building that was both welcoming and inspiring. If she could afford it, she would happily decorate her entire house with the items sold at the boutique, but that wouldn't be happening anytime in the near future. Her girls were growing like weeds and it seemed like she was spending her extra cash on new shoes or coats every couple of months. But a person needed a little pick-me-up every now and again, so she settled for buying the occasional small piece of bric-a-brac on payday and being thankful that she had a full-time job with benefits.

In fact, it still amazed her that Danielle had offered her the job in the first place, since she and Grady had once been engaged and it hadn't ended well. But Danielle was now married to a great guy, and Grady was engaged to Lex, a partner in the business. A convoluted state of affairs, but the end product was that Danielle and Grady were both blissfully happy and Annie had a job she loved.

"You're here early," Danielle said as she walked into the back room carrying a vase of wilted roses.

"The girls managed to get ready for school on time. I've worked up an incentive plan."

"Clever mom." Danielle gave her kind of a goofy smile.

"What?"

She bit her lip then blurted, "I'm pregnant! I'm going to be a mom, too!"

Annie gasped then reached out to hug Danielle, who was almost bouncing up and down with excitement. "When?"

"January."

"And no morning sickness?" Danielle shook her head. "Lucky you," Annie murmured. "I think I was sick for five months."

"Have I mentioned that I'm excited?" Danielle said. "I've been looking at Western baby stuff. A lot of it. You may have to rein me in so the store doesn't become Annie Get Your Baby Gear."

Annie laughed. "I'll do my best, but baby gear mania is like a sickness. Everything is so cute."

"I know." Danielle opened the cooler and took out the bouquet of flowers stored inside and replaced the roses in the vase. She jerked her head toward the boutique. "I have more news."

Annie followed, waiting until Danielle had placed the flowers on the end of the tall counter where they transacted business. She nodded at the locked door on the west side of the room. "I negotiated with Great Granny and because they're having trouble renting that little space after the Book Nook closed, she's letting me have it for a song. I'm making a quilt room." She walked over to the door and turned the old-fashioned key resting in the lock then pulled it open. The Book Nook had been vacant for almost as long as Annie had worked for the store, and the room was both musty and dusty.

Danielle stood for a moment, studying the space. "Definitely some work ahead of us." She glanced over at Annie. "If there is an us. I was wondering if you wouldn't mind putting in some overtime and helping me clean and paint this space. The cleaning we can do when we have downtime during the day, but the painting—I don't want fumes, so I figured that could be done during the evening. Thus, the overtime."

"I'd just do it," Annie said.

"I don't want you—"

"You can buy me a drink sometime. After..." She patted her abdomen.

"If you're sure," Danielle said, stepping farther into the room.

"Totally sure." Annie crossed over to the windows, which had brown paper covering them. "It'll be nice to get this paper down."

"It was never meant to be up for so long," Danielle agreed. "And it'll be nice not being next to a vacant space." She turned in a circle. "I'm going to hang the best quilts, put racks over there and see if I can score some dressers to display smaller items."

"I've been trying to make smaller items," Annie said. "I don't seem to have the knack." But she wished she did. Lex made metal jewelry for the store, and Kelly, who'd worked there before Annie, still brought in her pottery pieces. Annie had nothing to contribute.

"You know, I'm fine with you simply being a great associate."

Annie gave a soft snort. "I want a talent like everyone else."

"Maybe you're really good with interior paint," Danielle said with a wry smile.

"I do sling a mean brush." She did. The house she'd grown up in had been grim when she'd moved back home after Wes had left her. She and Grady had rented it out while she'd been in college and the renters hadn't been all that careful with the place. It'd taken Annie a long time to brighten the house with paint and small touches, making headway whenever her budget allowed.

"I was thinking Friday evening to paint? You can bring the girls."

Paint and her twins were usually an explosive combination. Annie lifted an eyebrow, thinking that Danielle had a learning curve ahead of her. "That sounds great and since its Friday, I think that would be a good night for the twins to spend the night with friends."

THE DAYS PASSED SLOWLY. Trace saddled up every day, exercising each mare in turn and even giving the cranky old gelding, Snuff, a go. After the daily ride, he worked out as best he could, read, watched videos and wished that Lex had a less meticulously cared for ranch. A guy named Hennessey had a practice pen nearby and Trace thought he might check it out, but knowing himself as he did, he didn't want to be tempted to hurry things along. The longer he healed, the better his chances of having a winning season the next year—and the better his chances of getting the best of Brick and funding that season. Or at least part of it.

The problem, as he saw it, was that the only way to be a successful bull rider was to live and breathe the sport. Unfortunately, that made downtime difficult. Trace had nothing to fill the hours once he'd gone through all his exercises and rehab, mental and physical, and fed the animals. The one positive to the ranch was that for the first time in forever, he had a real kitchen to work in—one where his stepmother wouldn't instantly kick him out, anyway—and within a matter of days his simple meals became more elaborate.

Being at the stove reminded him of being with his mom. As she'd grown more ill, he'd taken over the cooking, following her instructions as she sat at the table and watched, sometimes with her head resting on her arms. She hadn't had much of an appetite by that point, but she'd taught him to make hearty food that would feed a growing kid. She'd also taught him how to stretch ingredients, shop sales, use coupons and maintain a household budget.

Trace's mouth tightened as he put a cast-iron pan on to heat. He missed his mom. Sixteen years and the ache was still there. He'd lost his father not that long ago, but mostly he felt resentment when he thought of his dad. It wouldn't have killed the guy to open up a little—at least tell him he had a serious heart problem. But no. He didn't find that out until the heart problem had put his dad in the ground.

Lex had a nicely stocked kitchen and Trace started a list of the things he needed to replace as he used them. She also had a decent collection of cookbooks, and it was while he was thumbing through one, looking for inspiration, that he stumbled upon the Gavin chamber of commerce pamphlet and discovered that he knew a local bar owner. Gus Hawkins was also from northern Nevada, and he and Trace had competed in a lot of the same rodeos in high school and college.

It would be great to see someone he knew. Someone he didn't have to fake small talk with. For all of the time he'd spent alone in his life, alone on this ranch felt different. It had to be because he wasn't traveling and he wasn't riding bulls. His life had changed radically after the surgery and his brain was still trying to figure out how to cope with these new limitations.

TRACE DID HIS grocery shopping Friday evening, just before the store closed for the night, then parked outside the Shamrock. The place was beginning to get crowded, but there were still a few empty tables around the periphery of the room. Trace bypassed the tables and headed to the bar, which was manned by an older guy who looked at him over his glasses as he approached.

"Hey." Trace put his hands on the edge of the bar and looked at what was on tap. He ordered then asked if Gus was around.

The old guy's glasses slipped a little lower as his chin dropped. "It's his day off."

"I rodeoed with Gus during high school."

"You did, now?" Trace started to pull out his wallet but the bartender waved his hand. "First one's on me."

Trace smiled. "Thanks. I guess I'll stop by on a day that's not Friday."

"Or Thursday. His other day off. By the way, I'm Thad. Gus's uncle."

"Trace Delaney."

"You ride bulls."

"I do." He wasn't a big name, but it wasn't unusual for people who followed bull riding to know who he was.

"Are you done with the circuit?" Thad pushed a foaming draft across the bar.

Trace raised his glass. "Bad shoulder. I should be good to go in a matter of weeks." Months, he reminded himself. No pushing this recovery as he'd always done in the past.

"It's got to be rough on the paycheck being out for so long."

"Doesn't help," Trace agreed with a "that's life" smile.

A group of six or seven youngish guys dressed in matching baseball shirts came in through the back door, and Trace stepped back as they crowded up to the bar. "I'll tell Gus I saw you," Thad called as he backed away.

"Thanks." The place was filling up, but Trace found a quiet table near the empty pool tables, where he sat and slowly sipped his beer, watching the people around him. He was in no hurry to get back to the lonely farm and was therefore in no hurry to finish his beer. It was only 7:30 p.m., so a long night stretched before him.

Another rowdy group of kids dressed as cowboys came into the bar and soon commandeered the pool tables. Trace watched the dynamics in the group, pegged the cocky guy with the black hat as the leader and wondered if he'd looked that stupid after having one too many. A girl in tight silver pants draped herself around Black Hat, who practically shook her off. Silver Pants pouted a little as Black Hat took his pool shot then gave a smirk when the ball hit the edge of the pocket and rolled to the center of the table.

"I told you to rub me for luck," she said.

And Trace had had about enough people-watching.

He went back to the now almost deserted bar to drop off his glass, and he and Thad started talking again. Thad seemed fine to talk despite being busy at the bar, so Trace lingered a bit before heading out the back door leading to the parking lot. He'd barely stepped outside when he heard a woman cry out and then the sound of a scuffle. He rounded the first row of vehicles in the lot and saw Black Hat and Silver Pants standing next to a tricked-out truck.

"Leave me alone," the girl yelled. Black Hat didn't move, so she started slapping at him, until he put his hands up and pushed her back into the truck. Her head struck the mirror, and even though she didn't appear to be hurt, Trace started toward them. If it had been a couple of evenly matched guys, it would have been different, but this wasn't an even match.

"Mind your own business," the guy growled, barely sparing Trace a glance as he faced off with the girl who was now spitting curses at him while rubbing her head with one hand.

Trace stepped in between them. "She asked you to leave her alone."

"You going to get involved, cowboy?" the guy asked in a deadly voice.

Trace took another step forward, hoping the woman had the good sense to take off while she could. "I don't want to get involved, but if she wants to go—" Something hit him hard on his temple, knocking him sideways. His teeth clacked together and he tasted blood, but he didn't go down.

"You get away from us," Silver Pants shrieked. When Trace turned toward her, the guy swung at him. Trace managed to pull back enough to miss the brunt of it, but the guy swung again, hitting him square in the bad shoulder as he attempted to dodge the blow, and the fight was on. Trace got a couple punches in with his right hand before the guy grabbed his shirt and swung him around. He lost his balance and went down, pulling Black Hat with him.

They rolled in the gravel, hitting one another, the girl shrieking and smacking at them with her purse—the same purse she'd used to coldcock him. Just when Trace got a lucky shot to the jaw, he heard the sound of tires on gravel, and then the reds and blues lit the ground nearby. A pair of rough hands pulled him away from Black Hat and the next thing he knew, his hands were cuffed behind his back, the pain in his shoulder so raw and deep that he could barely catch his breath, much less give his name when the cop demanded it.

"He started it," the girl sobbed. "He did. We were out here talking and he just attacked us!"

Trace let his cheek drop to the gravel. He was so thoroughly hosed.

Chapter Three

"We need to give a statement," Danielle said as the deputies finished handcuffing the two men who'd been fighting in the parking lot behind the store, not far from Annie's car.

"Not until they get Shelly under control," Annie muttered back, even though she agreed wholeheartedly. They'd come around the corner just in time to see Shelly Hensley wallop the guy who'd tried to intercede on her behalf. Typical Shelly move. As the deputy turned her around to cuff her she loudly cursed him out.

"I think it's safe now," Danielle said.

Annie nodded and they started across the lot. The deputy looked over his shoulder at them as they approached, and she saw that it was Cullen McCoy, whom she'd gone to school with. "We saw the whole thing," Annie called as she and Danielle stopped a safe distance away.

Shelly glowered at her in a way that made Annie glad they'd waited until the cuffs were on. "They did not."

Cullen gave his head a tired shake, giving Annie the impression that it wasn't the first time he'd dealt with Shelly. Another cruiser pulled into the lot and after a brief conference with the female deputy who stepped out of the car, Cullen jerked his head toward the street. "I'll talk to you one at a time. You first." He pointed at Danielle, who followed him a few yards away.

Annie stayed put, shifting her weight and thinking that this was the most excitement she'd had since the girls let the snake loose in the house. The female deputy put her hand under the still-handcuffed rescuer's arm and when she helped him to his feet, a sound of pain escaped his lips.

Annie's mouth fell open, then she snapped it shut again. The guy who'd gotten creamed trying to help Shelly was Trace Delaney.

TRACE GLANCED PAST the female deputy to see who else was witness to his humiliation then swallowed a groan. A leggy blonde woman and…Annie Owen.

Excellent.

Shaking his head, he looked down at his boots, tightening his jaw against the pain shooting through his shoulder. To his left the woman he'd tried to help was spewing venom, and to his right the deputy who'd cuffed him was talking to the blonde. He had no idea where Black Hat was, but his hat still lay in the gravel close to where they'd fought.

He sensed Annie moving, cast another quick look and saw that it was her turn with the deputy. When she'd finished, the deputy came toward him.

"I'm going to ask you to take a breathalyzer test," he said after checking Trace's identification.

Trace nodded. He was more than willing to take the test—not that he had much choice in the matter. They'd draw blood if he refused. He blew into the tube and a moment later the deputy unlocked the cuffs.

"Hey! What about Danny?" Silver Pants shrieked before the female deputy took her by the arm and hauled her a distance away.

"Do you know these two?"

"No." And he knew better than to give more information than was asked for.

"What happened?"

"I was on my way to my truck and these two were dusting it up. The guy laid hands on the woman and I told him to stop."

"Did you threaten either of them?"

"No. I just told him to leave her alone."

"According to the witnesses," the deputy said to Trace, "the female suspect struck you without provocation and then the male suspect—" he glanced down at his notes "—took a swing and from that point on you were acting in self-defense."

"The guy in the black hat pushed her against the truck and she struck her head on the side mirror. She didn't appear to be hurt, so I thought I'd distract him so she could leave." His jaw tightened. "She chose not to go."

The deputy gave a weary nod. "I'll be dealing with both of them. Her for battery on you. Him for battery against both of you. Do you want to press charges?"

Trace shook his head. He just wanted to forget the evening, and he really wanted Annie to leave.

"Then you need to head on home." The deputy gave him a long, hard look. "Are you okay to drive?"

"I only had one beer."

"I'm talking about your injury. Maybe you should go to the ER. Get checked out."

"It's an old injury. He didn't do it."

"He didn't do it any good, either," the deputy said, shaking his head again.

"I'll take him home."

They both turned to see Annie standing a few feet away. Trace's chin jerked up. Yeah, as if he'd let her. He'd had his quota of embarrassment tonight.

"He got his head pounded against the ground at one point," she told the deputy. "Pretty hard."

That'd happened early on. She'd seen the whole thing.

"I'm fine."

Annie merely raised her eyebrows at the deputy, who then nodded. "Yeah. Take him home. Thanks, Annie."

Thanks, Annie. Trace's mouth tightened, but there was no good to be had from arguing with the law, so he started for his truck.

"My car is over here," Annie called.

"Her car is over there," the deputy echoed. Trace reversed course and by the time he got to Annie, she'd finished saying a few words to her friend and pulled the keys out of her pocket.

"It won't kill you to accept a ride home," she murmured. "I'll help you get your truck in the morning."

And the only thing that kept him from arguing was the fact that, yeah, he was starting to feel a little light-headed. He knew that feeling. Knew it well, actually. It happened when he got clocked too hard in the arena. It'd pass, but maybe he should be grateful instead of all surly. So after he scrunched himself into the front seat of Annie's car, he said, "Thank you."

She snorted a little and started the engine. "Right."

"No. Really."

She shot him a look then shook her head.

"What?"

He saw a corner of her mouth tighten. "No wonder Grady asked me to keep an eye on you. You're here less than a week and you've already tangled with Shelly Hensley."

"What a minute." Maybe he'd been clocked harder than he thought. "Why would you need to keep an eye on me? Grady asked me to keep an eye on *you*."

"Whatever." She slowed to a stop at an intersection then continued on out of town.

Trace fell silent, irritated, his shoulder throbbing. They rode for several miles and it wasn't until they got close to his place that Annie said, "Hey," in a somewhat grudging voice.

He glanced at her, frowning.

"He didn't tell me to keep an eye on you. He said you might need a contact in the community. You did. It all worked out. And I know that he asked you to keep an eye on me. He told me."

Trace nodded instead of answering.

Annie pulled into his driveway and then stopped next to the front walk. "Is everything really okay?"

"I just got beat up by a douche bag. What do you think?"

Her expression softened an iota. "If you need anything, will you call?"

"Like what, Annie?" It was the first time he'd said her name out loud and it sounded oddly intimate. She seemed to think so, too, because those blue eyes widened then narrowed.

"I don't know what your needs are," she said calmly.

He did and he was beginning to feel a need directed toward her, despite the humiliation of the evening. He had to get out of there. He reached for the door handle. "I'll figure out a way to get my truck."

"Or I could pick you up on my way to work at eight."

She was challenging him. Trace rarely if ever backed down from a challenge. "Thanks."

"Common sense wins. Cool." She gave her slim shoulders a shrug and despite the pain beating through him, and the very real concern that he'd set his rehab back by a week or two, Trace found himself wanting to smile.

ANNIE TOLD HERSELF—firmly—that there was no need for her to feel self-conscious about picking up Trace Delaney and giving him a ride to his truck, which was parked where she parked every day. It was the natural thing to do. The neighborly thing to do.

They were kind of neighbors…several-miles-apart neighbors, but they had the same zip code.

She pulled her car up to the gate at the end of Trace's walkway. The dogs shot out from behind the house, leaping up and down, their heads appearing and disappearing from behind the fence, and a few seconds later Trace came out of the house, looking dark and withdrawn.

He held his shoulder stiffly and his arm wasn't in his jacket sleeve, which concerned her, but having grown up a bull rider's sister, she didn't say a word about it and pretended not to notice the grimace of pain that flashed across his face as he got into her car.

"Thanks for doing this," he said politely as he folded himself down into the seat. Apparently he felt self-conscious about being ferried back to his truck. Men.

"Not a problem."

Once Trace was in the car and the door was shut, Annie couldn't decide if the car was too small or if he was too big. Only he wasn't big. He was tall and lean. Wiry, as bull riders tended to be. But the car felt different with him in it.

And whereas he'd smelled like a guy who'd been fighting in the parking lot the night before—which Annie had been surprised to find she didn't mind one bit—today he smelled of soap and man. She didn't mind that, either.

She bit her lip as she stopped at the end of the driveway. Since Trace seemed to prefer silence, she decided to honor his wishes and not make small talk. She did enough of that in the line of duty and it really wasn't that bad driving in silence.

He was the one who finally spoke as they hit the Gavin city limits. "Do you want to bring your girls to ride sometime?"

She sent him a frowning look, wondering where that had come from. "They can wait until Lex comes home."

"Yeah. Well, I've never spent time around kids, so I kind of panicked when they asked, but after you left I realized that I really had nothing to do with the matter. So, you're welcome to come…if you still care to."

There was something in his voice that had her glancing away from the road to him. "You're hurting and the last things you probably need are a couple of rowdy—"

"Annie." She shot another look across the small space. "I'm not the kind of guy who usually fights in parking lots."

Annie's eyebrows shot up as she realized what his concern was. "I wasn't worried about that." She let out a huff of breath. "Besides, I saw what happened. Shelly attacked you from behind when you were trying to help her. And you know what?" Another quick look his way. "You could have taken that douche bag despite your shoulder. He was tiring, you know."

She pulled into the lot and parked in her usual spot, fifty yards away from where his black truck stood close to the Shamrock. When she turned to take her purse from the backseat, she saw that he was studying her with a bemused look.

"I grew up with bull riders. You think I haven't seen a scrap or two in my day?"

She pushed the door open and got out. Trace did the same and she realized that perhaps she'd accidentally discovered the secret to feeling more comfortable around a guy who was putting her totally on edge. Treat him like her brother.

He smiled at her then over the top of the car—a slow smile that made Annie's nerves start to thrum.

Uh...no...the brother thing wasn't going to work.

It had been a nice idea, but she was going to have to come up with something else. She managed a look of concern.

"Are you sure about this? You won't feel invaded?" Because she thought he would, and pointing that out might be a great way to sidestep this rather generous offer.

"It's not my place. If the girls want to ride, they're welcome. I'll probably stay in the house, out of the way."

Annie lifted her eyebrows. "More likely out of harm's way."

"Well, like I said, I have no experience with kids."

Annie fought with herself. He was being nice because of what had just happened between them and the words "no, thank you" would solve her problem nicely and put *her* out of harm's way.

"How about Sunday at ten o'clock?" she heard herself say.

"Sunday at ten o'clock," he echoed. Then he gave her a quick nod before starting for his truck.

And Annie gave herself a moment to watch him go.

Chapter Four

Late Saturday afternoon, on the day after he'd gotten walloped in the parking lot, Trace went back to the Shamrock. He wasn't one to avoid a place just because he'd gotten the snot beat out of him there—if he were, he wouldn't be a very successful bull rider—and he wanted to say hello to Gus. He pushed through the door and saw Gus behind the bar and no sign of Silver Pants or Black Hat.

"Delaney!" Gus spotted him before he was halfway across the room and came out from behind the bar to meet him. "I'd man-hug you, but I don't know what part of you hurts."

Trace laughed as they shook hands. The truth was that his shoulder hurt like crazy, and he was concerned about the number of weeks he'd put himself behind in rehab by butting his nose into someone else's business.

"Let me buy you a drink," Gus said as he headed back around the bar. "Or better yet, wait five minutes until I'm off shift and I'll join you."

"Sounds good." Trace headed over to a table by

the door. Five minutes later Gus showed up with two frosted mugs of beer.

"I don't usually end my day this way," Gus said as he raised his glass to his lips almost as soon as he sat down. "But there are days." He took a drink. "Speaking of which, I heard what happened with Shelly last night."

"I imagine most everyone has heard by now."

"Pretty much," Gus agreed. "My uncle banned her from setting a foot in the place for a month about an hour ago. She threw a fit, so he made it two months and if she shows up before that, he'll call the sheriff and ban her for life." Gus gave his head a quick shake. "You have no idea the trouble that woman can cause." He smiled a little. "No. I guess maybe you do."

"Firsthand," Trace agreed. "If she's such a trouble-maker why not ban her for life now?"

"Because her father is—" Gus made quotation marks in the air "—important."

"He must be very proud of his daughter."

"Unfortunately, I think he is."

Trace gave a soft snort. What would that have been like? To have a father who was proud of you?

"Sorry to hear about *your* dad," Gus said, keying in to the direction of Trace's thoughts. "Gramps mentioned that he'd passed and that the ranch was for sale when I spoke to him a couple months ago."

"Yeah. Well, as you know, we weren't that close." Not even close enough for the old man to let his first-born know that he'd suffered two heart attacks before the one that had killed him.

Would it have changed anything? Trace didn't know, but at least he would have had the option of going to see him. Making peace. Although that was probably a pipe dream, because his father's wife would have figured out a way to keep him from seeing the old man, just as she'd driven a wedge between them when he'd first moved in with them after his mom died and his dad was still trying to figure out how to deal with the uncomfortable situation.

Trace had no idea of what she'd been afraid of—him usurping her boys in their father's affection? As if that would have happened. His younger half brothers had still been in the cute kid stage when Trace had arrived in Oregon. He'd been the gangly, awkward kid. Nothing cuddly and lovable about him. Maybe she'd simply disliked him because of what he represented. It didn't matter. She'd made his life a misery, but the result was that he had a great bull-riding career because of her.

Trace lifted his glass. "It still hurt to lose him." It had. There was no longer the slightest chance of them ever making peace, and deep inside him there was still a bit of the kid who wanted his dad to want him. "So how long have you been here in Gavin?" Trace asked, shifting the subject from himself.

"A matter of months. My uncle needed help and I'd just hit a wall in my career."

"Bad wreck?"

"Cranky old piebald named Murph stomped the living crap out of me. To the point that I decided it was time to hang it up."

Trace rolled his shoulder, testing for pain. "I'm not to that point yet."

"You'll know when you are." Gus spoke with quiet certainty that Trace found unsettling. Gus had been one of the most fearless riders he'd ever known. "And until then—" Gus raised his glass "—best of luck."

Trace returned the salute and stretched his stiff leg out. It felt good to talk, even if he did not care to dwell on the subject of retirement. The conversation shifted to Trace's current standings and his hope to compete in a few events prior to once again taking on Brick in Man vs. Bull, and Gus spoke about reestablishing a life after his own career. Trace knew that was something he'd eventually have to deal with, but he wasn't yet ready to abandon the sport that had made him feel as if he were someone, regardless of what his family had thought of him. Not even close.

After a good hour of talk, the place started filling up with happy-hour drinkers, and even though he wasn't wild about going back to the lonely farm, Trace paid for the second round and headed out. He rolled his shoulder as he walked to the truck. He and pain were old friends—competitors, really. So far he'd won every bout, and he had no intention of going down in this one.

Twilight had fallen and the automatic lights in the parking area were coming on. The lot was emptier than it had been when he'd first pulled in. People had gone home from work, but it was still too early for the bar crowd to come out en force. Annie's car was parked at the edge of the lot, right where it had been the night before when she'd all but frog-marched him to the vehicle. She kept late hours, but he imagined that in a town the size of Gavin, jobs were not easy to come by and she didn't have a lot of choice in hours.

He was almost to his truck when a door in the brick building at the far side of the lot opened, and Annie came out with a bundle of what looked like white sheeting in her arms. She carried it to the Dumpster and awkwardly attempted to push the lid open far enough to stuff the bundle in.

"Need help?" Trace called.

Annie gave a start then let out a breath, her shoulders slumping with relief when she recognized him. "Wouldn't mind," she said. "These things are kind of gunky."

He crossed the distance between them and lifted the heavy metal lid. Annie shoved the bundle in then wiped her hands down her pants. Pale orangish-colored streaks followed her fingers down the denim.

She grimaced at the paint stains then looked back up at him. "Hanging out in parking lots again?"

He smiled in spite of himself. "On my way home, actually. I figured if I'm going to live in this area for a while, then I should probably get back on the horse... or in this case go back into the bar."

"You should be safe enough now. Shelly got banned." She took a backward step, started to put a hand on her upper arm, then hesitated as she caught sight of it. Annie was not a neat painter. "I knocked a can over," she explained, even though he hadn't asked. "I caught it pretty fast, but not fast enough."

"You're a painter?"

"I am tonight. My boss is pregnant and paint fumes bother her, so she took the kids and I'm painting our new quilt room."

Okay. Explanations given. Dumpsters dealt with. Time for him to leave.

Except...he didn't feel like leaving.

He glanced over at her car. "I suppose you have to get right home."

"That was the plan, after I tidy up a few more things."

Trace cocked his head at her, going with instinct instead of common sense. "Would you like to go get a quick drink?"

A surprised look crossed her face and he thought for sure she was going to say no, but she gave a small shrug. "Sure. I haven't had a free evening in a long time." Trace started to smile and then she ruined it by saying, "And you are a friend of Grady's."

Yeah. He was. And he was finding Grady's sister... interesting.

She looked down at the paint on her clothes then grimaced at her hand. "I have to tidy up and change. Do you want me to meet you at the bar?"

Obviously she was not inviting him to come into the building with her. "No. I'll wait for you here."

"All right. I'll be fast." She gave him a pert look over her shoulder as she started for the door. "Try to stay out of trouble, okay?"

He found himself smiling again as she disappeared inside. Less than five minutes later she came back out the door, wearing a denim skirt, a red shirt, Western boots and silver beads. Somehow she managed to look both cute and sexy. The tiny smudge of apricot colored paint on her wrist only added to the package.

"You are fast," he said as they started across the lot.

"One of my many mother superpowers. I learned to dress on the fly as I averted disasters here and there."

"Broken water pipes?"

"I was thinking more along the lines of spilled milk."

Trace escorted Annie into the Shamrock, stopping at the bar long enough to order a draft for Annie and a sparkling water for himself while Annie claimed a table.

"Thankfully the music hasn't started," she said as she adjusted her chair. "Which means we can hear one another."

"Makes for better conversation," Trace agreed. And he was hoping for better conversation. All of his meetings with Annie had been strangely awkward up until now.

Annie smiled a thank-you as the server placed the beer and water on the table. She met his eyes and he said simply, "I've had two drinks and I'm driving."

The corner of Annie's mouth tilted and he thought she was going to say something about him showing remarkable common sense for a bull rider, but instead she said, "It's going to be strange going home to a quiet house." She lifted her beer and reached over to tap his glass lightly with hers. "Thanks for helping me delay the moment."

"Anytime." He meant it.

Annie took a small drink then set the mug down as

a young guy in a Western shirt approached the table. "Hey, Annie," he said, barely sparing Trace a glance. "I haven't seen you in a while."

Her expression became polite but cool as she said, "I haven't been out in a while. The kids keep me busy."

The guy turned his attention to Trace, smirking a little before he looked back at Annie and said, "Good thing there're no women with big purses here."

Annie smiled sweetly up at him. "Cody, have you met Trace Delaney? He's watching Grady's place."

The kid's mouth fell open as he recognized Trace's name, but before he managed to say anything, Annie said to Trace, "Cody rides bulls. Does pretty good, too."

"I, uh…" Cody had gone red now that he realized who exactly had been walloped by Shelly. He pushed his hands into his back pockets then pulled them out again. "Good to meet you. I didn't recognize you. Probably because I didn't expect you to be here. In Gavin, I mean." He shoved a hand at Trace, who took it gamely. "I only ride on the local level. Nothing like…yeah." He shifted his weight. "Any chance you might be interested in going to Hennessey's practice pen? Maybe give some pointers?"

"Will there be any women with big purses there?" Cody went even redder at the jab and Trace felt kind of bad for him. "I might be able to find some time."

"Thanks. That would be…great. Thanks."

"See you around," Annie said gently and Cody took the hint, heading back toward the bar where his small group of friends waited.

"You play hardball," Trace said once Cody was out of earshot. The kid had definitely been territorial about Annie, but the feeling was not reciprocated. Annie looked more annoyed than anything. The color was high in her cheeks and her full mouth had tightened again. He felt a strong urge to do something about that. Annie needed to relax a little.

"Cody is the little brother of one of my high school friends, and has had a burning crush on me forever. Even the twins didn't slow him down." Annie focused on her hands before bringing her blue gaze back up to his. "That sounds kind of vain, doesn't it? But it's the truth."

Trace smiled. "Nothing wrong with speaking the truth." And he could totally understand the kid having a long-lasting crush on Annie.

She settled back in her chair. "Here's a bit more truth… It feels kind of unreal sitting here and having a beer instead of racing home—even with the girls at Danielle's." She took another small drink, then put the mug down. "If you weren't a friend of Grady's I wouldn't be."

He'd gotten that idea earlier, when she'd agreed to go for the drink.

"Why's that?"

"I don't go out much."

"Homebody?"

"Exhausted," she said candidly. "To conserve energy, I rarely stray from my normal routine, which consists of kids, work, kids." She smiled at him then gave her head a small shake as if suddenly realizing how small her world was at the moment.

"Their father doesn't help?"

She raised her eyes. "I haven't seen their father since before they were born."

Okay, then. "That's pretty far out of the picture."

"He sends checks quarterly. Automatically, through his bank."

Trace knew from his own experience that checks weren't enough. Not even close. But Annie wasn't ill, as his mother had been, and her life did appear to revolve around her girls.

Annie smiled ruefully and echoed his thought. "You'll have to forgive me if I talk about my kids a lot. They're pretty much the center of my universe."

"Maybe it's good to focus on yourself every now and then."

"Voice of experience?" she asked drily.

"Touché." He reached out and touched her hand, barely aware of the action until he felt her silky skin beneath his palm. "And don't get me wrong—I'm all for putting your kids first. My mom tried to do that, but she was too sick to do it well. She died when I was fourteen."

"I'm so sorry." Annie drew her hand back in a smooth motion as soon as he lifted his.

Was she afraid he'd touch her again? It had been meant as a friendly gesture, but the contact had sent an unexpected jolt of deep awareness surging through him. He wondered if she'd felt it, too, or if he was the only one feeling this strong pull. Life would probably be simpler that way, and, frankly, he couldn't read her.

"Where did you go after she died? Relatives?"

"My father's place. He was kind of a distant relative." Her eyes widened at his response, and Trace sucked in a breath. That had sounded awful and he hadn't asked her to have a drink with him to rehash his past…or hers, for that matter. "I didn't have a lot of contact with him before that. I barely knew the man when I moved to his ranch."

"That had to be rough."

He smiled as carelessly as he was able. "It got me into bull riding, so no regrets." Except for never really knowing the guy who'd given him his name.

"Your dad taught you to bull ride?"

He managed not to snort at the idea of his father spending that much time with him—or his stepmom allowing it. "The neighbor taught me. I used to go hang out there…long story." One he didn't feel like telling, so instead he smiled, watched as her gaze traveled over his face, wondered what she saw there. A winner? A loser? A guy who considered his father a distant relative? In many ways he was all of the above, but when he'd asked Annie to have a drink with him, he hadn't expected the conversation to take this route. Judging from the speculative expression on her face as she studied him, neither had she.

"I hadn't meant to get all serious," he said.

"I don't mind serious."

"What do you mind?" he asked, more to fill the silence than anything.

"People who say things they don't mean and make promises they can't keep." She spoke lightly, but there was an underlying edge to her voice. Annie had some hidden scars, and he assumed they were related to the father of her twins.

"I tend to err in the opposite direction," Trace said with a touch of irony. "I tell people things they don't want to hear."

Annie raised her glass in a mock salute. "At least they know where they stand." After taking another small drink, she asked, "Why'd you ask me out for this beer, Trace? Because I get the feeling from our first encounters that you're more of an introvert than an extrovert."

So much for faking small talk. But at least her question had an easy answer. "Opportunity to get to know you better."

The color rose in her cheeks, but her tone was matter-of-fact when she said, "You couldn't have done that tomorrow?"

"I thought it might be easier alone."

"You're right. It is." She pushed her half-finished beer aside. "You're really okay with the girls coming over to ride tomorrow?"

"I don't mind."

"You say that now."

He smiled at her. "You know, Grady never came out and said it, but I think he did want me to keep an eye on you—" Annie's expression cooled, but he put a hand up before she could speak "—not because you're not capable, but because he's your brother."

Annie rolled her eyes toward the pressed tin ceiling. "I know. He was gone for almost two years, building his career, and I think it still bothers him that he came back and the place was in pretty bad shape."

"It looked all right to me."

"Smoke and mirrors. The house is old, and while I'm fairly handy with repairs, I have this thing about power tools, so I'm not much of a carpenter." Her mouth tightened ruefully as she spoke, as if having a thing about power tools was somehow embarrassing. "It's the ear-splitting noise, I think, and the possibility of cutting off a digit, so I never learned to use anything except a cordless drill. There's only so much you can do after a tornado with a hand saw, a hammer and a power drill."

"You had a tornado?"

"Damaged two of the outbuildings. Thankfully, the girls and I were in town at the time. Grady came back to put them together last spring."

"We were all surprised that he chose to leave the series." He'd been healthy and riding well, but had made it clear that his family needed him.

"I think the time off did him good. He's riding better than ever."

That he was. Trace checked stats frequently, which only fed his growing impatience to get back into the series even if his chances of qualifying for Nationals were next to none.

Annie didn't finish her beer but she told him it was because she drank so rarely that she was now officially a lightweight. After Trace walked her to her car, she smiled up at him. "Well, friend of Grady's. Thank you for the drink."

Friend of Grady's. Again.

"Anytime." He touched the brim of his cowboy hat and then waited for her to unlock her door before heading to his truck. As he unlocked his own door he couldn't help but wonder why she kept laying down that boundary. Was it for him? Or for her?

Chapter Five

Annie told herself that there was no reason that she should feel an edgy sense of anticipation as she picked up the girls at Danielle's house prior to taking them riding on Sunday morning…but she did. The girls raced for the truck, backpacks bouncing, thrilled that they had back-to-back big events—being spoiled rotten at Danielle's followed by horseback riding—while Annie hefted the large tote bag they'd left behind.

"This seems heavier than before."

Danielle smiled. "I cleaned out my costume jewelry last night. I had a lot of help."

"I bet." Annie shifted the bag to her other shoulder. "I had a beer with Trace Delaney last night." She figured she may as well come clean, since Danielle would get wind of the matter before the close of business on Monday. "We met by accident in the parking lot after I finished painting."

"Again?"

"Yes. Strange, huh?" Annie shifted the bag then forced herself to hold still. "You should see the quilt room. It's gorgeous. Great color."

Danielle gave her a wry look. "I can't wait."

"Don't read anything into this," Annie said darkly. "The beer, I mean."

"Why would I?"

"Because I haven't been out with anyone forever?" Not since she'd given in and gone on a blind date arranged by well-meaning coworkers at the library where she'd worked part-time. "I only went because he's Grady's friend." And her casual mention of her night out was turning into a case of she-doth-protest-too-much. So she shut her mouth.

"See you tomorrow," Danielle said on a note of gentle amusement.

"Right. Thank you. For everything."

"Mom, I'm going to need new boots," Katie announced as Annie got into the car. "My toes are touching the ends."

"Mine, too," Kristen added, as if that wasn't a given. Her girls were truly identical, except in temperament.

"Noted," Annie said. She'd try to squeeze boots into the next paycheck, which meant nothing was allowed to break down. Nothing beyond her fix-it capabilities anyway, such as the furnace, which had made a funny noise that morning. After she'd turned it off and pushed the reset button, it'd whirred back into action without so much as a hiccup, warming the house against the spring chill, so she hoped that was merely a fluke. The washing machine had given her no further problems now that it had its new hose. It was too warm for the pipes to freeze and her mechanic had just given her faithful little car a clean bill of health—in return for the promise of a bounty of harvest from her garden during the summer. Marlo did love fresh tomatoes.

She turned into Lex's driveway and the twins instantly undid their seat belts and leaned over the front seat, pointing at the corral.

"Look! Mr. D'laney has the horses caught," Katie said from behind her.

He also looked pretty spectacular standing next to the fence, wearing worn jeans, a blue plaid flannel shirt and a black Carhartt work vest. Annie's throat went dry. The guy was not only handsome, he was built, too. Long-legged. Lean. And those shoulders...

He'd looked sexy at the bar last night, which was one reason she hadn't finished her beer—she'd wanted to keep her inhibitions firmly in place—but in the light of day...oh, yeah. He truly was something. One of those guys who got better looking each time you saw them.

Last night while they'd talked, she'd dealt with the fact that for the first time in a very long time, she was physically drawn to a man. And since that man had no idea as to the direction of her thoughts, she'd allowed herself to enjoy the feeling. It was delicious, dangerous, a touch bewildering—*Why now? Why this guy?*— but she saw no reason to fight it because all it would ever be was a feeling. The twins bouncing in the seat behind her were walking, talking reminders of where her priorities were centered for the next several years. As far as Trace Delaney was concerned, she was simply Annie Owen. Sister. Mom. Chauffeur to injured parking lot fighters.

Annie turned off the ignition and opened her door

as the twins spilled out of the passenger side. "Hi," she said as Trace approached, congratulating herself on sounding so amazingly normal and unaware of the fact that he looked like he'd just stepped out of a hot cowboy Pinterest board. "Thanks for catching the horses."

"I didn't know what you wanted me to do ahead of time, so I brought the horses in—except for that gnarly gelding. I couldn't see any reason to have him in the corral."

"Snuff?" Annie asked on a laugh. "He's Lex's dad's old horse. He runs the pasture in pretty much the way Lex runs her farm."

"I noticed." He smiled easily, meeting her gaze and holding it for a few long seconds. Annie wondered how she remembered to breathe. He'd been sexy in the bar, but in the light of day...

A tug on her sleeve snapped her back into mom-mode. "Can we catch Daphne and Lacey?"

"Good idea," she said, shifting her attention to Katie and Kristen. The girls exchanged happy looks and headed for the tack shed as Annie followed.

"I hung the halters on the fence," Trace called.

The twins didn't look back, but they instantly changed course as they spotted the halters hanging from the fence posts. They climbed the fence rails to take the halters down and were back on the ground by the time she and Trace caught up with them.

The old mares were already ambling toward the gate before the girls got it open. "It's a good sign when the horses come to the riders," Trace said.

"They have a good relationship. And the mares get a lot of loving out of the deal."

And he was supposed to be hiding out in his house while they were there, not standing next to her, smelling all delicious. Anyway, that had been the impression she'd gotten when he'd extended the invitation—pre-drink. Had the drink changed things?

Annie pushed her ponytail over her shoulder and chanced a glance at the man. Trace smiled a little and then Annie turned her attention back to the girls and called, "Watch the lead ropes, ladies." She looked back at Trace, a matter-of-fact tone in her voice as she said, "Lex doesn't like the lead ropes dragging in the dirt. She had the girls wash them in a bucket of soapy water the last time."

"She runs a tight ship."

"The girls loved it so much they want to wash lead ropes every time we come."

"Well, they can certainly wash lead ropes today if they so desire."

"We probably won't have time for that."

"Tight schedule?"

Annie gave Trace another sidelong look before focusing back on the twins, who were leading the mares back to the gate. "I have a lot to catch up with on Sundays, so as much as I'd like to avoid my chores, I probably shouldn't."

"I wish I had that problem." Annie frowned at Trace and he said, "I like to keep busy and Lex didn't leave me much to do."

Annie laughed. "You should come by my place."

She regretted the words the instant they left her lips. He really shouldn't come by her place. She cleared her throat. "Keeping up with the laundry is a two-man job sometimes." Her attempted save sounded lame at best.

How was it that she'd held her own last night in an unfamiliar environment even as she became more and more aware of how attracted she was to him, but now, in the light of day, in a familiar environment, she felt so self-conscious?

Maybe because of that dream you had about him last night?

Annie felt color creeping up from her neckline. She couldn't remember the particulars, but there was no question as to who the hero of the dream had been. And now that she was close to him, it was almost as if it had really happened.

She was having a morning-after moment.

Get a grip. This is not *a morning after.*

"Are you all right?"

"Hmm?" She innocently shifted her gaze to his handsome face.

"I thought you might have forgotten something the way you were frowning."

"No. Trust me. I've forgotten nothing." It was all coming back in Technicolor detail. Unfortunately.

He nodded and she smiled at him and hoped it didn't look too strained. "I actually enjoy doing laundry when my washer doesn't attack me." It was true. There was something soothing about sorting and washing clothes.

"Laundry isn't my strong point. I never have been able to get the arena dirt out of my jeans."

"Same with Grady. He really grinds that stuff in."

"The trick is to hit the ground on your feet after disembarking. Then your jeans don't suffer."

Annie narrowed her eyes. "How often does that happen?"

"Every now and again." He opened the gate and the twins led the old mares out of the corral. Annie helped with the bridles, and Trace threw the small saddles up. The girls then led the mares to the edge of the fence where they scrambled up and expertly leaped onto the horses' backs.

"They seem at home in the saddle," Trace said as they started riding down the path toward Lex's training arena. Without Lex or Grady there to ride with them, the twins knew better than to ask to go out on the trail.

"Do you horseback ride?" Trace asked as they followed the girls.

"Not much."

"Bull ride?"

She smiled. "I stopped at calves." She moved past the girls to open the gate and they rode into the railed enclosure.

"Tell us what to do," Kristen said.

"Circle with the rail on your right," Annie called. She glanced over at Trace. He seemed almost shy around the girls, as if he wasn't quite certain how to deal with them, but showed no inclination toward leaving. "If you have something else to do…"

"I don't."

Her eyebrows lifted at his instant response.

"Well," he said with a tilt of his head, "I don't get

to do a lot of talking here, except to the dogs. And I enjoyed talking to you last night."

An unexpected sensation of warmth flowed thought her. "Did you know you'd be isolated when you agreed to watch the place?"

"I did. But I've never been in a situation where I had nothing to do. Usually I'm traveling and when I'm not, I lend a hand on the ranch where I stay and train during my time off—or I used to, anyway. The ranch sold, so here I am."

"Reverse," Annie called to the girls. The mares changed direction and Annie noticed that it was with very little effort on the part of her daughters. Katie hadn't even moved her reins. The mares knew the voice commands—as well they should, given the amount of time the girls spent riding with Lex.

"I know that you guys don't get much time off in the bull-riding schedule. Other than for injury, I mean." Grady had a couple of months off in the summer and then the series had begun again in August.

"I like it that way. I've never been one to stay in one place for long."

"Even as a kid?"

"No," he said softly without looking at her. "As a kid I stayed put for the most part. The only problem was that it wasn't in places where I wanted to be."

"That's too bad."

"That's life." He gestured at the arena when Kristen was looking at her over her shoulder.

"Trot," Annie called. The old mares broke into a slow jog and she glanced back at Trace. "I bet you can't wait for that shoulder to heal and to get back to your life."

His expression said more than words. It was killing him not to compete. Grady was the same way. Silence fell between them and Annie did her best to focus solely on her girls, but it wasn't easy when she was so aware of the guy leaning on the fence a few feet away. And even more difficult when he said, "Would you like to go riding sometime?"

Annie shot him a sideways look as red flags started to wave furiously. "Is that an invitation?"

"It is."

All right… She hadn't seen this coming. "Because you're looking for company?"

"Partly."

"The other part?"

His gaze traveled over her in a way that warmed her. "Because I wouldn't mind going riding with you."

Her heart gave a couple of slow thumps as she grappled with this unexpected development. "I don't know." She spoke honestly. "I'm a full-time mom with a second full-time job."

"No time for riding."

She went with the truth. Not sugarcoated. "No time for complications."

"Meaning me?"

She felt the color rise in her cheeks. What if she was reading this all wrong? "I'm going to be honest here. I'm rusty."

"Rusty?"

"I can't tell what kind of invitation you're offering—"

She looked over at the girls, who were shifting impatiently in their saddles, waiting for a new cue. "Reverse course and walk."

"I'm offering a friendly invitation with the full understanding that you are a full-time mom with a full-time job and no need of complications. I also understand that the girls would be along for the ride. Literally."

She felt a smile forming on her lips, but she wasn't certain why.

He smiled back. "Let's go for a ride next weekend. You, me and your girls. We can follow the trail into the mountain. I'll bring lunch." He didn't move closer, but it felt as if he had when he quietly repeated, "No complications."

Annie pushed her windblown tendrils that had escaped her ponytail back from her face as she fought with herself, trying to come up with a viable reason to say no. "Next Sunday?"

"Next Sunday."

"Mo-om!"

Annie turned back to the arena and rested her arms on the second highest rail, her heart beating just a little faster as she called, "Figure eight at the jog!"

She wanted to go for this ride with Trace. It astounded her, but she did. "All right," she heard herself say. "It's a date."

"Mom, the furnace is making that noise again."

Annie hated that noise. After resetting the furnace the previous weekend, the old beast had run well for almost forty-eight hours. Then it had made the noise again. Annie had pushed the red button and restarted the furnace, only to have it make the noise twelve hours later. Then six. Today she'd turned on the heat immediately after they'd returned home from riding—two hours ago.

The heating system in her house was clearly edging toward a major problem, but it wasn't there yet, which left Annie in a conundrum. Should she call in a repair guy now, three weeks before payday? Or check out a fix-it book from the library and tackle the repair herself? Fix-it book and positive thinking were her go-to options, but honestly? She was a little afraid of the furnace. Moving parts she didn't mind. Moving parts that involved flames—not a fan.

"Did you hear me, Mom?" Katie called from the living room, as if the clattering wasn't readily apparent.

"Thanks, honey. I'll take a look." *Push that red button. Hope for the best.*

She headed down the cellar steps, which no longer creaked under her weight, thanks to Grady. He'd done a lot of much-needed carpentry around the place when he'd returned home last summer to repair the tornado-damaged outbuildings. He'd also offered more than once to help her financially, but Annie didn't feel right taking his money. She'd made her choices in life, just as he'd made his. Not that she was unhappy with her life…she just wished she had more earning power—but that was what happened when one dropped out of college due to an unplanned and difficult pregnancy. Earning power decreased and she didn't see a whole lot she could do about it until the twins were older. In the meantime, she'd be thankful that she had a job she loved, which paid the bills—as long as there were no unexpected ones—a place to live and healthy girls.

She'd also hope that the heating system held out until payday so that she could hire a bona fide repair guy instead of doing it herself.

Annie crossed the basement thinking that the furnace didn't seem any happier to see her than she was to see it. The rattling sound intensified as she came to a stop in front of it.

"Three weeks, okay? I'll turn you on only when it's absolutely necessary to warm the house. Just...hang on, okay? Because if you don't, then I have no choice but to try to fix you myself and I don't want to do that."

After the pep talk she turned off the power, turned it on again and the furnace began to hum as if it were brand-new. Annie suspected it was faking her out and that in a matter of an hour or two it would once again make the noise. As it turned out, she barely made it upstairs before the hum turned into a rattle. She crossed the room to the thermostat and turned it off with a snap of her wrist. The rattling stopped and the house was quiet—for two whole seconds until a squeal erupted from one of the bedrooms. A happy squeal, which again reminded Annie to count her blessings.

She went back to the cupcake batter she'd been in the middle of making when she'd received the furnace alert and lost herself in the soothing routine of baking. She'd just opened the oven door to pop in the first batch when Kristen appeared in the kitchen doorway.

"Mom?"

Annie looked over her shoulder before sliding the pan into the oven. "Yes?"

"It's getting cold in here."

"Put on a sweatshirt. We're giving the furnace a rest."

Her girls exchanged looks. "For how long?"

"Until ice forms."

The twins' eyes widened—with excitement rather than alarm. Annie laughed, thinking that she needed to take a more childlike approach to the adventures of life. Ice-skating rink in the kitchen? Not a problem. She crossed the room to wrap an arm around each girl, hugging them close. "Kidding. But we're only going to run the furnace a little bit because of the noise. I'll get the heaters out of the shop, but we can't run them full-time because they—"

"Eat dollars?" Kristen asked.

Annie hated that the girls had heard her say that enough that they could repeat it, but facts were facts. The heaters did eat dollars. "Pretty much."

"That's okay, Mama. We're tough."

"Girls can be tougher than guys, you know," Kristen added. "Uncle Grady told us we were way tougher than him when he had to take the slivers out of our feet. He said that he had to get an'thesia to have his slivers taken out!"

Annie smiled as she got to her feet. A bit of an exaggeration, but she did appreciate his encouraging the girls' toughness factor.

"Why don't you two find your boots and put them

away so that we can find them easily next Sunday?"
The day of the big trail ride. The no-complications
trail ride. Oh, yeah. Annie had the feeling that she
was standing at the top of a slippery slope and getting
a little too close to the edge. But was she backing up
an inch or two in the name of safety and sanity? She
was not.

"We already know where our boots are. And we
polished them," Kristen said. "Does the furnace mean
we can't get new ones?"

Stab to the heart. "The weather is supposed to get
really cold over the next few weeks. We might not be
able to ride for a little while, so let's wait and see."

"All right." The wistful note in Katie's voice pushed
the knife in a little deeper, but facts were facts. Warmth
before hobbies. At least their other shoes still fit.

"Be honest with me…are your toes just barely
touching the end of the boots, or are you curling them?"
Because the girls had definitely curled their toes to
stay into favorite shoes even when Annie could afford
to replace them.

"Barely," the girls said in unison and Annie had no
doubt that they were telling the truth. Okay…maybe
the furnace parts wouldn't cost too much and maybe
she could squeeze the boots into the next budget and
in the meantime they could wear their old ones.

Think positive.

"Do you want us to polish your boots?" Kristen
asked as she lugged the polish box out of the pantry
and Katie started to spread the newspaper to protect
the floor.

"I'd love it," Annie said. It was a ritual Grady had started with them to help contain their preriding excitement, and now they wouldn't dream of heading to Lex's farm without polishing first.

Annie reached for her sweatshirt hanging by the door and shrugged into it. It was getting cold fast, which meant that she needed to find the heaters and start burning some dollars.

THE NEXT MORNING the house was frigid when Annie got out of bed. She turned on the thermostat and instantly turned it off again as the grinding rattle started. Okay. Heaters it was.

She knew from past experience that she couldn't run electric heaters for three weeks without taking a huge hit to her wallet. The money would be better spent on the furnace itself. The question was how much was the part and what would the repair cost with labor?

With Danielle's blessing, she left work two hours early on Monday, picked up the girls from Emily's house just as they arrived there from school and headed off to the public library where she found her favorite fix-it book on the shelf. Flames aside, it would definitely be cheaper to figure out the problem, order the part and attempt to fix it herself. Worst-case scenario, she'd have to hire Marlo to install the part she was going to order from him.

"Again?" the librarian asked as Annie set the heavy book on the counter to be scanned.

"Furnace this time. Last time it was a faucet." Small

potatoes compared to a furnace, and no flames involved.

"If we ever cull this book, I'll save it for you."

"I would love you forever."

Annie took the manual to the children's section and read while Katie and Kristen chose books. By the time they were done, Annie had come to the conclusion that the blower motor was losing a bearing. Of course she would have to replace the entire assembly. She stopped by Marlo's Small Engine and Appliance Repair on the way out of town and asked if he could order the part for her.

He made a quick phone call then said, "I can have it by Saturday."

She could last until Saturday.

"I thought you were afraid of tackling the furnace."

"Economics have changed my mind."

"I wish you luck." Marlo shook his head. "I don't like working on oil furnaces. Too temperamental."

"Tell me about it," Annie replied, ignoring the small twist in her gut at his words.

"I'll give you a call when the part comes in."

Annie patted the counter. "Thanks, Marlo."

"Annie?" She turned at the door. "If it's just the blower motor assembly, you shouldn't have a problem. It's the burners that I hate working on."

"Then let's hope it's the easy fix." The three-hundred-dollar easy fix—and that was with Marlo charging her his cost for the part, despite the fact that she'd offered to pay more.

"Can you fix it, Mom?" Katie asked when Annie got back into the car.

"Not until Saturday when the part comes in."

Kristen counted on her fingers. "Five days of eating dollars."

"Let's be thankful it's not six," Annie said as she started the car.

"Or seven," Katie said.

"Or seven," Annie agreed with a smile. Or eight or nine or ten.

Chapter Six

Annie Owen's daughters were beyond cute. Trace hadn't spent a lot of time around children—and next to no time around them in a one-on-one manner—and even though he was still a touch intimidated by the twins, he assumed that if he treated them like small adults, he'd be okay. So far it seemed to be working.

"Mr. D'laney," the twin in the blue coat—Katie?— said in a serious tone, "you gotta be careful saddling Lacey because she blows."

"Would you like to walk her while I saddle Snuff?"

The twin took the reins from him and started leading the old mare in a circle while Trace tossed the saddle up on the cranky old gelding he was going to ride. Trace was well aware that the mare blew— puffed out her belly when being saddled, which resulted in a loose cinch later—but it impressed him that the little girl was aware. Both girls took their horsemanship extremely seriously.

Annie was busy saddling Daphne for the twin in the red coat, while her own mount pawed the ground impatiently, digging a good-sized hole. Trace gave Snuff a pat on the rump, intercepted the twin leading Lacey in a circle, stopped the mare and quickly tightened the cinch.

"I think we're set."

The girl put her fingers under the cinch and pulled, testing the snugness, then gave an approving nod. Trace fought a smile as she said, "Would you hold my horse's head while I mount?"

"At the fence?"

"Yes." He held the mare's head while the twin clambered up onto the fence and leaped into the saddle. The mare twitched an ear and Trace handed the girl the reins.

"Katie, right?"

She beamed at him. "I'm the blue twin. Kristen is the red twin."

"I can remember that. Katie Blue."

Annie's mare pawed nervously as she helped her other daughter into the saddle.

"When's the last time you rode?" he asked, nodding at the impatient pinto mare.

"I can handle her."

Trace took her at her word. The mare he'd borrowed from Cliff, the neighbor who usually took care of Lex and Grady's chores when they were on the road, was fresh off pasture and hadn't been ridden in a while. He'd planned to ride her until Annie told him that she'd prefer not to ride Snuff.

He waited to mount the gelding until Annie was in the saddle, just in case. The pinto skittered and danced and threw her head, but Annie sat deep and Trace decided to keep his mouth shut rather than offer once again to trade mounts.

The ride up the trail took longer than it did when Trace rode it alone, but he liked the slower pace, liked listening to the girls chat with one another and talk to their horses. Big plans were discussed—tree forts, their future as ropers and barrel racers—as well as social issues—the mean kid in first recess and whether the best teacher was Mrs. Bell or Mrs. Lawrence.

"I have them in different classes," Annie explained.

"How's that working out?" Annie's mare had settled almost as soon as they'd hit the trail and she'd had to work a little.

"They weren't at all in favor at first, but now they can tell each other about their day... I think it's working out. Or I'm scarring them for life. One or the other."

Trace grinned at her. "They look pretty happy to me. I think you're doing something right."

"I hope so. It's a crap shoot each and every day."

He'd never thought about how much time and effort went into managing kids and helping them grow into adulthood, possibly because he'd never been managed.

They finally reached the clearing near the top of the first ridge and dismounted. Katie explained to Trace that he shouldn't tie his horse up by the reins and he agreed that was a good rule to follow.

"So you really haven't spent much time around kids?" Annie asked when he passed her the sandwich bag before sitting on a granite stone a few feet from the one she sat on. The girls had already taken a sandwich each and abandoned them while they scaled the mini boulders behind them.

"Be careful," he and Annie said together, then he shook his head as he opened his sandwich.

"Next to none."

"You seem to know what to say and when to say it."

"I guess I'm treating them like regular people."

"Kids appreciate that," Annie said. "Good sandwich. What did you put in the tuna fish?"

"Minced capers."

She peeled open the edge of the sandwich and took a look at the filling. "I've never heard of that."

He gave a small shrug. Neither had he. It was simply something he'd tried once and liked, so he continued to do it. "A little lemon juice, too, but just a touch."

"Are you some kind of fancy cook?" It almost sounded like an accusation.

He shook his head. "Not even close. I just kind of like messing around in the kitchen. Some things come out better. Some worse. The only person I feed is myself, so I can afford to experiment."

"My fan base doesn't appreciate experimentation unless it's with frosting and sprinkles. All the mainstays…those have to be the same every time or I hear about it."

"Tough crowd."

"You have no idea." Annie finished her sandwich then folded the plastic wrapper and tucked it into her jacket pocket. "What else do you do besides cook?"

"I ride for eight."

"And when you aren't doing that anymore, what will

you do?" He didn't answer immediately and she asked softly, "Do you have a plan?"

He swallowed the unexpected dryness in his throat. "I do not. I'd like to continue doing something related to bull riding." As would most of the guys in the sport. "Working for a stock contractor or a bull-training outfit."

"Much future in that?"

"You mean like 401(k)s and stuff like that? I don't know. I don't have any real commitments, so as long as I put money away for a rainy day and food on the table, I'm good."

He had the strong feeling from the ironic look that crossed Annie's face that she'd heard those words before. Grady? Or perhaps the father of her kids?

Annie let out a low whistle and pointed behind him. He turned and saw that bluish-black clouds were rolling in at a remarkable speed.

"We better get moving," he said. A gust of wind hit him as he spoke.

"The weather does change rapidly here, but this wasn't due in until tomorrow."

"I think it's here now."

Annie called the girls while Trace untied the horses. Rather than leading the mares to the rocks as the girls wanted, he tossed them up into their saddles and then mounted. Annie's mare was once again dancing, but she turned her in a couple of tight circles and the little horse decided that maybe she didn't mind walking quietly, after all.

"Can't really blame her," Annie said as they started down the mountain. "Wind gets my blood up, too."

The wind did more than get the blood up as they headed down the mountain. It cut through Trace's jacket and blasted down his back. The girls were leading the way, their old mares walking more quickly than they had on the ride up the mountain. Horses tended to move faster going home, but Trace had a feeling that the old girls wanted to get back before the skies opened up. He wanted the same thing. A half mile from the farm, the hail started. Trace dismounted and helped the little girls off their horses, who had started to dance impatiently as hail balls ricocheted off their broad hindquarters.

"Let's walk for a ways, so the horses don't spook."

The girls agreed then put their chins down and started leading the horses through the bouncing hail balls. If it had been warmer, they probably would have stopped to play with them, but it was nowhere near warm. Trace's face was growing numb from the stinging ice balls, and even though they had big hoods with furry ruffs, he knew the girls had to be getting pelted, too. They didn't so much as whine.

The hail stopped as abruptly as it started and then the clouds opened, allowing shafts of light to shine through, tinting the landscape shades of amber and gold. The effect was breathtaking.

"And that's Montana for you," Annie said from behind him.

Trace tossed the girls back into their damp saddles and mounted Snuff. By the time they got back to the farm, the only sign of the storm was the melting hail balls that covered the yard.

The girls helped unsaddle their horses and brush them down, even though their little hands were red with cold.

"You did really good today," Trace said after the tack was put away and the mares released to the pasture.

"We're used to being cold," Katie said in an offhand way as the four of them walked to Annie's car.

"Yeah?"

He saw Annie flush, but before she could intercede, Kristen interjected matter-of-factly, "Our furnace doesn't work and the heaters eat money."

Trace shot Annie a look. "So you're going home to a cold house?"

"No," she said coolly. "I'll let the heaters eat some money when we get home."

"What's wrong with the furnace?"

"As near as I can tell, it's the blower motor."

"As near as you can tell?"

"I checked a book out of the library and there aren't really a lot of things that can go wrong with an oil furnace. I cleaned the filters and replaced the nozzle last week, but it's still making the noise, so now I have to explore more expensive options. I'm ninety percent positive that the bearings are going out of the blower motor."

He stared at her. "You haven't had anyone look at it?" He stopped next to Annie's car.

"Nope."

"I think I'd be hesitant to tackle a furnace." Of course, his mechanical abilities were pretty much limited to fixing the old baler on the ranch and changing the oil on his truck. He'd been too busy training to get too deeply into mechanics.

"My repair guy assures me that this is a simple transplant operation."

Uh-huh. "Would you like me to stop by while you do this operation? Just in case…?"

"Just in case of what?"

"You need someone to hold the book open to the right page or something?" He wasn't about to say because he didn't like the sound of her tackling the furnace alone or to ask if Grady knew she was doing this repair. He liked his head right where it was, on his shoulders, instead of being taken off.

Her expression shifted, and was that a flash of relief he saw? "I can't say that I'd mind some backup. I have more than just myself to think about." She shot a look over the hood of her car where the twins were digging patterns in the gravel with the heels of their boots.

"And I don't mind backing up. Not one bit."

"I was going to tackle it today."

"How about I follow you home?"

"Yeah. How about that?" she asked wryly, but she smiled at him, taking the sting out of the words, and Trace found himself feeling pretty good about that. Maybe too good.

"I'll take off as soon as the operation is over. You don't need to worry about what to do with me afterward."

"Am I that transparent?"

"You're cautious, Annie. You have to be." As if to punctuate the remark, the girls laughed and crouched down to start building a path through the wet gravel for a slow-moving beetle that had just come out of hibernation. "You have more than yourself to look out for."

"There was a time when I wasn't so cautious," she said in a low voice. "Kind of got myself into a situation because of it. I can't afford to do that again."

He reached out and touched her, brushing his fingers against the smooth, cool skin of her cheek without thinking. "I understand."

She didn't look as if she fully believed him, but she didn't move away from his touch. Slowly he dropped his hand back to his side. "I'm only here for a matter of months, Annie. I like spending time with you, but I will not push my way into your life. I don't make promises I can't keep."

"Hearing that makes me feel better," she admitted. "I have too much at stake to play games."

As she drove home Annie seriously debated as to whether or not she'd fallen victim to temporary insanity when she'd agreed to let Trace follow her home. Or was it hormonal insanity?

She most definitely wanted someone there while she did the blower-motor transplant. For safety. So why had she invited the man most dangerous to her peace of mind?

He's only dangerous because you don't trust yourself.
No, she did not.

She'd spent most of her twenties raising little kids and ignoring men and sexual urges and now, *boom*! It was as if everything had been quietly building inside her and was now seeking release.

Well, it wasn't going to happen anytime soon.

The girls were happily planning their next mountain excursion—warmer coats and gloves were mentioned, as well as emergency survival rations—and seemed oblivious to the mini panic attack their mother was having.

Drawing in a calming breath, Annie loosened her death grip on the steering wheel and told herself the damage was done. Trace was coming to her house—in fact, he was right behind her, so now she had to work with the situation.

This isn't a big deal. Not as big as she was making it in her head. And she was only making it a big deal in her head because Trace Delaney was playing hell with her hormones…but he didn't know that. He would never know that.

But you are still taking a chance by letting him come home with you!

By the time she got home, Annie was totally on edge. The girls undid their seat belts and piled out of the car while Trace parked his truck several yards away, as if he was afraid that Katie and Kristen would dash in front of him if he parked any closer. She kind of appreciated that.

"When you get done helping our mom fix the furnace, do you want to play games?" Kristen asked Trace as she skipped alongside him on his way up the walk.

He shot a look at Annie, as if seeking reassurance, but before she could save him, he came up with his own answer.

"That sounds like a lot of fun, but I have chores to do before dark, so today's not a good day."

"Well, maybe another time," Kristen said easily.

Annie opened the door and Trace reached over her to take hold of the edge, holding it while the girls walked in under his arm. Once inside, he took off his hat and glanced around.

"I've never seen the place dry."

Annie couldn't help but smile.

"It hasn't been wet in *days*," Katie told him proudly.

"True story," Annie replied. The house felt different with him there, just as her car had felt different. *She* felt different…and as she went for her tool kit, she couldn't help but wonder whether she had the same effect on Trace.

TRACE FOLLOWED ANNIE down the stairs into a neatly kept stone-walled cellar. There were wooden shelves along the two side walls, which held rows of home canning. Along the wall opposite the staircase stood a hot water tank, a small chest freezer and the oil furnace.

"Are you ready for this?" he asked as she set her book and a box on the freezer. He put the tool kit he carried for her beside the box.

"No."

He smiled but did not reply. After flipping off the main electrical breaker and then testing the circuit to make certain it was indeed dead, Annie propped open the book, opened the tool kit and then pulled the new blower motor out of the box. Trace glanced over the book while he waited for Annie to familiarize herself with the new motor, and decided that it was a fairly straightforward job. He had a feeling her mechanical abilities exceeded his own, so he saw no need to offer suggestions simply for the sake of conversation. With a frown of concentration creasing her forehead, Annie removed the old motor, disconnecting wires and unfastening the mounting screws. Once it was free, she looked it over and then set it aside.

"I can't tell you how much I hope this is the problem because if it isn't, then I haven't got a clue."

She picked up the new motor and proceeded to wire it in and then screw it to the mounting.

When she was finished, she wiped her hands down the sides of her jeans and then carefully set the screwdriver and socket set back into her toolbox.

"This is the scary part," Annie said as she went back to the breaker box. "I have this fear of wiring something wrong and setting the house on fire. That's why I have more than the average amount of smoke detectors."

"It didn't look like there were too many areas for you to mess up on this job."

"No, thank goodness." She flipped the breaker and then punched a red button on the furnace panel. A few seconds later the pilot lit and then the furnace came to life. "My other fear is that the furnace will somehow catch fire. It's not logical, but it concerns me."

"It seems to be running well," Trace said.

"It always ran well right after I restarted it." She dusted her hands off then glanced over at him. "This was easier than I thought it would be. I'm sorry that I dragged you over here."

He wasn't. "Better safe than sorry."

"Maybe."

"I had nothing better to do."

"If you say so."

"I like watching you work."

"Mmm-hmm."

"And I promised I would take off once the furnace was running," he added.

Was that a whisper of disappointment he read on her face?

Maybe…

The girls were waiting at the top of the stairs when Annie opened the cellar door. They high-fived their mom, and Trace grinned as they went to stand on the heater vents when the furnace began to blow.

"No more dollar eating," Katie announced.

"Just the normal amount of dollar eating," Annie corrected before shooting a look Trace's way.

Dismissed?

"Well…those chores are waiting," he said.

"We can play a game next time you come by," Kristen assured him.

Trace crouched down in front of her, feeling only a little awkward as he said, "I look forward to that. And it was a lot of fun riding with you guys today."

"We're not guys. We're girls," Kristen informed him.

"I stand corrected," Trace said as he got to his feet. Tough crowd.

"I'll walk you to your truck," Annie said.

Escorted from the premises. So much for that whisper of disappointment he'd thought he saw cross her face. Maybe he was the one who was disappointed. But he'd promised to leave as soon as the furnace was fixed and he was a man of his word.

Annie slipped into her coat and followed Trace out of the house. The air was still brisk from the storm, but the setting sun cast warm golden light over Annie's neatly kept yard. Everything about her place was warm and homey, the exact opposite of what he knew when he'd been growing up. He hoped the twins would look back in the years ahead and appreciate the home their mother had made for them.

Trace stopped before opening his truck door and looked down at Annie, who was wearing a cool expression. The woman was hard to read. On the one hand, he thought maybe she liked him. On the other, she couldn't hurry him out of there fast enough.

"Thanks again," she said.

"Anytime." One corner of his mouth quirked up before he said, "I mean that, you know."

Annie's lips compressed and she nodded, then she raised her hand and brushed her fingers against his cheek, just as he'd done to her earlier. He felt his breath catch at the light touch. Then he captured her hand with his and leaned down to take her lips in a kiss that surprised both of them. And while the kiss had been soft, his body was now hard.

Annie dropped her hand and took a step back, her blue eyes wide and cautious as they held his. "I'll see you later." Her voice was a bit husky and she didn't wait for him to reply, but instead took another backward step then turned and walked briskly toward the house, leaving Trace staring after her.

Damn.

Chapter Seven

It all came down to what did he want and what did she want?

Annie sat up straighter and tried to pay attention to Brad Olsen, the Parent-Teacher Organization president, as he outlined the year-end school events. They'd just covered the lower elementary play and Annie had volunteered to help with costumes, and now it was on to career day. But despite her best efforts, her thoughts kept drifting back to the conundrum sparked by one simple kiss. A kiss she hadn't been expecting.

Her first kiss in what? Two years? Had it really been that long since she'd gotten an obligatory good-night kiss after an obligatory blind date with one of Danielle's friends? Yes. Two years and a few months.

So had it been just a spur-of-the-moment thing? Was Trace interested in exploring further? Was she?

It seemed as if she should know the answer to her side of the equation, but she didn't. Even though she had no definitive answer, she was becoming more and more aware of an urge to explore. To experience new things…or maybe even some old things she hadn't expérienced in a long time—like dating a guy she found attractive. Did she dare?

Annie was not going to overthink this…even though she'd been overthinking it all day. Now was the time to stop.

"What do you think, Annie?"

She jerked as the mother sitting next to her whispered her name. "I, uh, was a million miles away. I'm sorry."

"Brad just asked about canvassing the local store owners for prizes for the end-of-year family picnic."

"I can't do both costumes and canvassing," Annie whispered back. Last year she might have done both, but she had been working part-time at the library then. As it was, she was probably going to have to get help from Danielle to make butterfly costumes.

After the meeting broke up, Annie drove to Danielle's house to pick up the girls.

"Do you have time for a quick cup of tea?" Danielle asked. "The girls are helping Curtis in the workshop."

"I should get home." She was exhausted and looking forward to getting the girls bathed and in bed so that she could do the same.

"I hear you invited Mr. D'laney home to watch you work on the furnace," Danielle said, perfectly mimicking the girls' abbreviated version of Trace's last name with an amused lift of her eyebrow. "Funny, you didn't say anything about that today at work."

"It didn't seem important." Annie had been fairly certain that the girls were going to spread the word, but hadn't seen much she could do about it. Telling them not to say anything would have made them curious, which would have been even worse than their happily telling Danielle that she'd invited Trace to the house. "I wanted backup for the furnace operation and—" she shrugged nonchalantly "—he is Grady's buddy."

"Wise to have backup," Danielle murmured. "The girls said he didn't stay very long. They seemed disappointed."

"He stayed long enough," Annie said mildly and left it at that. She would love to pour her guts out to Danielle and ask advice, but she wasn't ready to do that just yet. There was still a chance she was misreading things.

He kissed you.

But still…

The girls burst in through the door, followed by a slightly bedraggled Curtis. Annie smiled at him as she put an arm around each girl. "Thank you for entertaining."

He gave her a rueful grin in return. "Good practice for the future."

Annie didn't have the heart to tell him that nothing could fully prepare him for the future. Parenting was a learn-as-you-go adventure, one she was still feeling her way along on. It was all trial and error and Annie was trying her darnedest not to make many errors.

Which brought her back to Trace. What to do, what to do?

When Trace got home after kissing Annie in her driveway, the first thing he had done was dig out the old-fashioned phone book and look up the number for Jasper Hennessey. If the man had a bull-riding practice pen, Trace wanted to be there, even if he couldn't ride. He had to do something to fill his days besides working out and thinking about Annie and what his next move—if any—might be.

He wasn't the kind of guy who just kissed women on the spur of the moment—especially a woman he wasn't even dating. He didn't know why he'd kissed Annie and he certainly didn't regret kissing her, but now he wanted to do it again and he wasn't certain following that road would be a good idea…although part of him said it was Annie's decision as to which road she wanted to take. She didn't want complications in her life, but she'd certainly kissed him back.

This was a puzzle he wasn't going to solve by kicking around the house. He wasn't going to solve it at the practice pen, either, but he could distract himself there. When he got hold of Hennessey, the man was more than welcoming, even when Trace explained that he wouldn't be taking part, but was going more to get out of the house than anything.

"Ri-ight," Hennessey said in a knowing way. "I heard you were in the area. I was hoping you'd call." He gave Trace the hours and days of practice and Trace told him he'd see him soon—as in that afternoon.

When he arrived at the practice pen several hours later, he walked into the covered arena, drew in the scent of dirt, manure and animal sweat and felt as if he'd come home. There was a small crowd of riders there and a couple of older guys, all dressed in old jeans and flannel shirts. The younger guys were wearing their protective gear and the older men had on cowboy hats and canvas coats.

"Hey," Trace said as he approached.

"You must be Trace," the taller guy with the silver mustache said, holding out a hand. "I'm Jasper. Good to meet you. Cody said you might stop by."

Trace smiled and shook hands, inwardly rolling his eyes at the bit about Cody. The kid probably hadn't mentioned that he'd all but kicked sand in Trace's face before discovering who he was. "Good to meet you." He looked at the handful of riders milling around, stretching and adjusting gear. Cody was there. He saw Trace, did a double take then dropped his chin and headed over.

"Glad you could come," he said with just enough self-deprecation in his voice that Trace decided that he was probably okay.

"Glad you told me about the place."

Trace went to lean on the rail with Jasper and Bill, his brother. Watching was going to be harder than he imagined. Rain drummed on the roof and Trace glanced up. "Nice to be out of the weather."

"I prefer the outdoor facility. We usually use it during the summer and fall. Just something about being out in the elements."

Trace knew exactly what he was talking about. Whenever he'd escaped the house during his teen years and headed out into the fields or mountains on horseback, the sting of the wind and the splatter of rain had always made him feel free and independent. He could think about the here and now, and not the cold feeling he got whenever he walked into what was supposed to be his home.

"I imagine if you see something, the kids wouldn't mind you pointing it out," Bill said as they loaded the first bull.

Trace wasn't much in the helpful hint department— not because he didn't want to help these guys. He did. It was because, honestly, what worked for one bull rider might not work for another. But there were some things that he'd mention if he spotted them. Bull-riding basics.

"You bet," he said before making a conscious effort to relax his tight shoulders and ease the knot out of his gut. What he really wanted to do was ride.

But it was better to feel antsy here than at home.

"How many butterflies need costumes?" Danielle asked as she handed the hammer up to Annie, who stood on a ladder.

Annie pounded in a nail to hold up a quilt rail before answering. "Fifteen."

"Wow."

Annie descended the ladder and studied the rail. Thankfully it was level. "I figured butterflies were easier than the squirrels and bunnies. I can find some big scarves and work from there."

"Great idea. We might ask Granny if she has any scarves tucked away in one of her trunks. I swear that she hasn't thrown out a piece of clothing in fifty years."

"I can't vouch for the safety of the scarves."

"Good point." Danielle folded a small quilt and set

it on an antique chair Annie had painted white after work the previous evening. "Maybe the thrift shops."

"That's what I was thinking." When she wasn't thinking about Trace, that is. She hadn't seen him in a few days, but he'd never been long out of her thoughts. Even this room reminded her of him, since she'd been painting it when she'd bumped into him behind the building for the second time in two days. It was like some cosmic force was pushing them together.

"Speaking of Granny," Danielle said, "Mom and I finalized the details for her birthday party and we managed to book the banquet room at the new pub. Will Emily babysit the girls?"

"Yes. It took me a while to convince the girls that a grown-up birthday party in a bar was not a place for a couple of seven-year-olds."

"I'll have to spoil them a little."

"As per usual," Annie murmured wryly. She moved the ladder to the opposite wall. The room was going to be beautiful, with quilts fully displayed on the two larger walls and smaller items arranged on tables, bureaus and chairs, as they were in the main store. All they needed were a few more pieces of furniture, which Annie hoped to find when she and the girls went to a farm auction that coming weekend.

"Oh... Brad Olsen from the PTO might call about—"

"Career day at the school," Danielle said. "I know. I met him at the bank. I encouraged him to ask the new owner of the little coffee shop. She's young and eager and has never been stared at by thirty kids who ignore your talk and want to know if you have any cats."

Annie laughed. Danielle had pretty much hit the nail on the head. Career day was more like Interesting People Day to the little kids. "Look at the time," Annie warned and Danielle let out a gasp as she saw that it was almost four o'clock.

"Good thing my OB always runs late." She headed toward the back of the store to gather up her purse and sweater. "See you tomorrow."

After Danielle was gone, Annie tidied up the store and then settled in the comfy chair near the counter and went to work on the cross-stitch kit she'd bought to fill her time when business was slow. She enjoyed the methodical process of pulling the thread through the canvas and watching the picture slowly take shape— *slowly* being the key word. This was not a hobby that would allow her to add stock to Annie Get Your Gun, but it kept her hands and mind occupied. For the most part. Except for those moments when a certain long-legged bull rider shoved his way into her head. And she just as firmly shoved him back out again. All this mental shoving was wearing on her. What was she afraid of? Why did she feel like she had to stop thinking about Trace?

The girls. Fear of messing with status quo.

Fear of the unknown.

As she saw it, she had two choices. She could either continue to dodge the issue and hope it went away, which it very well might—or she could confront it.

Ask him out.

Annie's needle paused above the canvas. Crazy idea. What would be her objective in asking him out?

She set the canvas in her lap and frowned at the opposite wall where a glittery portrait of Annie Oakley holding her rifle stared back at her. Did she have to have an objective? She was interested in him and maybe he'd been correct when he said that she needed to focus on herself every now and again. She picked up the hoop and jabbed the needle in. *Ask him out. Have a safe, friendly date.*

Safe? Why would she think that a date with a guy like Trace, who sent her hormones into overdrive, would be safe?

Because he said he kept his promises and she believed him. She didn't know him that well, but she sensed he wasn't by nature a liar.

And if he did lie to her, Grady would have his hide.

LATE WEDNESDAY AFTERNOON, just after Trace had finished feeding Lex's livestock, he was surprised to see Annie's car pull into his driveway. He was even more surprised to see that she was alone.

He crossed the wide gravel area that separated the house and barn as Annie parked. She got out of the car and came around to the front, coming to a stop a few feet away from him. She tilted up her chin and met his eyes, then pressed her lips together as if having second thoughts about whatever she was there to do. Something stirred inside him as he studied her face, remembering what her soft lips had felt like beneath his own.

"I've come to discuss...something." Color rose in her cheeks as she spoke, but her expression remained carefully cool. Matter-of-fact. Too matter-of-fact, which had Trace wondering what was coming next. Did she want him to babysit? Because while her girls were adorable, his kid skills were nil. Besides that, it would be so easy to do something wrong.

"What kind of something?"

She sucked a soft breath in through her teeth. "Would you like to go to an auction this weekend?"

"With you and the girls?" That would probably be lively, but he was game. And it would help fill an empty day.

She looked surprised then a little embarrassed. "No. I'm asking you out."

"Out?" He echoed her words as he tried to gain footing, determine if she meant what she was apparently saying, as in, she wanted to go out with him.

Her mouth hardened. "You know...like to keep company? Go out?"

"I understand what it means." Trace rubbed a hand over the back of his neck, feeling stupid and off center. "Sure. I'll go to an auction with you."

"I've surprised you," she said flatly.

"A little."

She shifted her weight and looked past him. "I'm new at this, so please excuse my awkwardness and feel free to say no." Her cheeks were on fire now, but she maintained that serene, distant expression that made Trace think she was dying a little inside.

"I thought you were rusty." She frowned, but before she could say anything, Trace reached out and took her wrist, gently easing her a couple steps toward him, and to his relief she didn't pull back. "When is your auction?"

"Sunday. I'm looking for some furniture for the store."

Those lips. Right there. He wanted to kiss her again, but was smart enough not to do it.

"But the only caveat is…" Annie held his gaze in a way that made him believe that she knew how tempted he was by her mouth. "I have to be careful of my girls. I don't want them to suspect…well…anything." The color in her cheeks was subsiding, but they were still stained pink. "Nothing can happen that might give them ideas—"

"Like me kissing you in the driveway?"

"Yes. Something like that."

"They didn't see, did they?"

"No. Thank goodness, because I would have had a lot of explaining to do."

Explaining she wasn't ready to do. He could see that. He wondered where she saw this thing between them going, and decided that she probably didn't know. She was well aware of the fact that he was pulling up stakes and following the circuit as soon as he was healed, so it wasn't like she didn't have full disclosure on that aspect.

Annie pulled back and he let her go, his hand falling loosely back to his side.

"You honestly want to go?"

He smiled a little. "What do you think?"

She gave a small nod instead of answering. "I need

to get back to town and pick up the girls. I'll see you Sunday? Eight thirty maybe? I'll drive."

"Wouldn't it make more sense for me to drive? I have a truck."

"So do I. Grady's."

"Sounds good, Annie. See you then."

ANNIE'S HANDS WERE shaking when she turned the key in the ignition. She glanced at her reflection in the rearview mirror as she pulled to a stop at the end of the driveway and was surprised at how cool and in control she appeared. Like a woman going after what she wanted. The only problem was that she didn't have a clear view of what she wanted, but she'd figure it out. As far as the girls were concerned, Trace was a friend of their uncle Grady's, who was making friends with their mom.

Would there be benefits involved in this friendship?

Way too early to be thinking that way, but still, the very idea of experiencing what Trace had to offer made her breathing go shallow. "No benefits" would be the sane way to go, but there was something about Trace that had her edging away from sanity and logic. Or maybe she was simply edging closer to something that she'd been subconsciously looking for and had just now found.

Take. It. Easy.

He's only here for a short time. Don't get in over your head.

It wouldn't be hard to do, getting in over her head. But she was an adult, who could make her own choices and deal with the consequences, as long as they didn't touch her daughters. Trace understood that, which was another reason she was going out with him. He got it.

Annie picked up the girls and they stopped at the drive-in hamburger place, newly opened after being closed for the fall and winter. Annie loved hot dogs with the works, but they were too hard to eat while driving, so she ordered the same as the girls—a junior hamburger—which allowed her to indulge in extra calories in the form of her first milkshake of the year.

"We should do this more often," Kristen commented from the backseat as she dug fries out of her bag.

Annie glanced at her daughter in the rearview mirror and smiled. They did *this* once or twice a month, and that was what kept *this* special.

Emily had been surprised when Annie had asked about Sunday babysitting, but she loved getting the hours whenever possible, thus boosting her retirement income. "We'll have a craft day," she said.

"They'll love that." And Annie was so very glad she hadn't told the girls she'd been thinking of taking them to the auction. That way there were no explanations, no hurt feelings. She might want to stretch her wings, go on a date or two, but not at the expense of her kids' happiness.

"We find out what our play parts are on Monday!" Katie announced as Annie pulled up to the mailbox next to the driveway. "We got to write down what we wanted to be on a list, but Mrs. Lawrence said we might not get the part we want. I want to be a butterfly because they're prettiest, but Shayla wants to be a bunny."

"She *has* a bunny…" Kristen said, her voice trailing off hopefully.

Annie chose to busy herself sorting through the mail rather than say no to the less than subtle hint that a bunny would be a welcome addition to their household. "I hope you are butterflies, because you can help make your costumes."

"Out of glitter and stuff?" Katie asked.

"Definitely glitter."

The girls instantly started planning what color costumes they wanted. Annie set the mail on the seat beside her and started down the driveway. Butterfly costumes and butterflies in her stomach.

Chapter Eight

It'd been a long time since Trace had cut himself shaving, but he nicked himself good less than an hour before Annie was due to pick him up. Cursing under his breath, he stuck a small piece of tissue on the wound and then shook his head at his reflection.

Why are you so freaking nervous? You're going out with a woman. You know...like you've done many times before?

But this was Annie and he had a make-it-or-break-it feeling about this first date. When was the last time he'd felt like that?

Maybe the high school prom.

High school. Yes—that nailed it down perfectly. He felt like a high school kid getting ready for a date. Ridiculous, but true. And it wasn't like it was a real date. It was a farm auction.

He grimaced at his reflection as he slapped tonic on the uninjured part of his face. Actually a farm auction was his idea of a great first date—especially when neither of them had any idea where this was going. Annie knew he was leaving; he knew that she put her daughters first in her life, but there was no denying the attraction between them. Exploring that attraction seemed like a good idea, as long as they were on the same page.

He had a feeling that he was Annie's way of sliding back into the dating world. A way to spread her wings and gain confidence with someone she liked, who wouldn't put pressure on her to take matters any further than she wanted. If she had started dating someone local, the girls would find out, but he was a friend of her brother's. The guy who was farm-sitting for a relative. They were probably safe enough from gossip. Probably. Small towns could be brutal.

He sat on the bed and slid his feet into cowboy boots. He'd spent a lot of time speculating as to Annie's motivation and agenda, but his own...no, he was clear on that. He wanted to spend time with an attractive woman. He liked Annie. And he needed to treat her well, or Grady would skin him. He smiled a little as his heel finally slipped into place in the boot. Maybe that was why Annie seemed to feel safe with him.

Trace was ready early and he found himself pacing near the front door as he waited for Annie to show up. The dogs sat in a row, their heads turning in unison to watch his progress across the floor and back again. Finally he let them into the yard, where they would spend the day, his head coming up as he heard a deep rumble in the distance.

Straight pipes. He hadn't heard that sound in a long time.

A few minutes later a classic Ford F-250 turned into

the driveway, its exhaust pipes growling. The truck had at least a four-inch lift and a weathered decal at the top of the windshield, pronouncing it to be a FORD. The rig was a teenage boy's fantasy and Annie looked darn cute behind the wheel.

"Grady's truck?" he asked when she rolled down her window.

"'Fraid so. He tricked it out in high school, and even though he promises to make it more adult every time he comes home, he never seems to get the job done."

"Sure you don't want to take mine?"

She looked tempted but shook her head and he understood. She wanted to have control. He could understand that. "Get in if you dare."

He dared. He went around to the passenger side and got in. Annie smiled over at him and put the beast into gear as he fastened his seat belt. She was wearing dark jeans and a simple white shirt under a short denim jacket. Her light brown hair was loose around her shoulders instead of in its usual ponytail and she smelled really, really good. There was also a touch of self-consciousness in her smile and he felt the same. In an odd way it was like meeting her for the first time.

She waited until they were on the county road before she chanced a glance at him. "I'm not going to lie. I'm nervous."

"Why?"

"Because this seems kind of official. A date and all that."

He shrugged one shoulder. "So it's a date. We're tough. We can handle it."

Annie laughed. "I guess." She slowed as a rabbit darted across the road ahead of her then stepped on the gas. The pipes rumbled. There was something about a small woman driving a big truck that Trace liked. A lot. He wanted to reach out and touch her, but a big tote bag was in the way, so instead he eased back in his seat and told himself to relax. His nerves were thrumming just like they did before a ride, and that was simply nuts. Annie kept lifting her chin, as if giving herself a pep talk, so Trace decided to come clean.

"I'm nervous, too."

She gave him a curious look. "Really?"

"Yeah."

A frown creased her forehead. "Somehow I figured a guy like you would have groupies. Grady used to."

"I'm not a big groupie guy, and having groupies isn't the same as going on a first date."

"Huh."

Fifteen minutes later Annie followed a line of cars into a driveway leading to a farm and parked in a field that was already filled with cars and trucks. When she turned off the engine, the world suddenly seemed a whole lot quieter.

"Next time we take my rig," he said with a wry smile.

"Then next time you do the asking," Annie replied, reaching for her door handle.

"Touché." And he kind of liked that she was talking about next time.

They ordered hot dogs just before the auction began

and Trace watched in amazement as Annie loaded the bun with everything on the condiment table.

"You're not going to be able to eat that thing," Trace said. "It's going to explode on you."

"Watch me," she said, a glint of challenge in her eye. She lifted the sagging bun to her lips, opened her mouth…then set the hot dog back in the cardboard container, reached for a plastic knife and cut a small piece, which she popped into her mouth.

"Hey. No fair."

"I broke a rule?"

"I think so. Since when do people eat hot dogs like that?"

"I hope the hot-dog police don't come after me." Her eyes sparkled as she spoke.

"You never know," Trace said before taking a bite of his own hot dog—the regular way. "We might not want to hang around, just in case you get reported."

"All right. I overloaded and I don't usually eat hot dogs this way," Annie admitted. "I didn't want to risk dripping mustard on my new blouse. But I do love a lot of stuff on my dog."

"Obviously."

They finished eating and then wandered through the farm implements and antiques. Annie stopped to inspect almost every piece of furniture, running her hand over the wood, studying the lines, looking for damage.

"Have an idea of what you want?" he asked, thinking again that this wasn't a bad way to have a first date. If it went bad, she could focus on the business at hand—buying furniture for her store. But it didn't feel as if it was going bad. It felt as if a steady vibe was growing between them, especially when they accidentally—or not so accidentally—touched.

"I've always wanted an old wagon," Annie said as they passed several old buckboards and utility wagons parked in a row. "By the time I get to the point that I can afford to spend money on something as frivolous as that, they'll be hard to find."

"We used to have old wagons on my father's ranch."

"Your family ranch?"

"It never felt like that," he said softly. "It was my father's ranch. I only lived there for a few years and I didn't really spend a lot of time there. I spent more time at the neighbors'. They took me under their wing and I learned to bull ride there."

"Did your dad watch you ride?"

"Only a couple of times. Local events. It would have looked bad if he hadn't gone." He gave Annie a serious look. "But you know what? That's the past. It's gone and I've moved on. Right now I'm here with you and I like it." Which made him just a little edgy. Being with Annie seemed pretty darned perfect—right now. When it was just the two of them in a different world than their own.

They finished the preview, then got bidding paddles and took their seats. The auction started not too long after that. Annie leaned forward as the first lot came in, then settled back when the bidding started. Trace leaned back, too, his thigh pressing lightly against hers as he stretched out his legs. Annie didn't move away until a bureau she'd had her eye on was brought up for bid.

Trace had never bid in an auction, but he could tell that Annie had. She looked relaxed, but her body was taut as she waited until the proper moment to enter the fray. She lost the first piece she bid on, but she won the next three.

"All I need to win now is that lot of three chairs."

"Good luck," Trace murmured. He enjoyed watching her, the way her chin rose when an opposing bid was acknowledged. She would be a terrible poker player, he decided. He also wasn't going to tell her that.

Annie lost the chairs and had started to pull her jacket back out of her giant tote bag, when an old wheelbarrow was brought in. She stilled, then took her paddle back up again.

"A wheelbarrow?" he asked. It wasn't old enough to be an antique. It was just…ugly.

"Shhh," she said gently, as if he were one of her kids, her eyes never leaving her prize.

Trace shushed and Annie bid. She won that thing, too. Cheap.

"I like to garden," she said when she finally met his gaze. "I need a wheelbarrow."

"That thing is not a wheelbarrow. It's a bunch of rust on a flat tire."

"It's also five dollars and that's what rust-killing paint and a tire-patch kit are for."

"I'll take your word on that." Trace had no experience with either. He'd never owned a bike of his own nor had he ever painted anything. His skills outside the arena were lacking.

With the help of the guys who were monitoring the purchases, Trace loaded two small tables, a bureau, a single high-back chair and a rusty wheelbarrow into Grady's truck without feeling so much as a twinge from his shoulder. Things were knitting together well, which made him feel hopeful that he'd be able to practice soon.

"Nice truck," one of the guys who'd helped them load said with a wink.

"Not mine," Trace was proud to say. He couldn't wait to make fun of Grady's wheels to his face the next time he saw him.

And when would that be?

Either when Grady came home or when they met on the road again.

"What now?" he asked as Annie tightened one corner of the elastic netting covering her purchases.

"Lunch and then I thank you for a great time and go pick up my girls."

"I get lunch?" he asked. "Two meals in one date?"

"The hot dog was a teaser. Besides, I'd love a beer before calling it an afternoon."

Trace agreed, because he wasn't ready for the day to be over.

"I'm on the clock, though," Annie said. "My sitter is booked until five this afternoon and then she has a function to attend. I can't be late picking up the girls."

Yes. They did live different existences in that regard. He was free to come and go as he pleased, and he liked that about his life. Liked not staying still for long and being able to do what he wanted to do when he wanted.

That was something Annie needed to know about him—something he needed to make clear from the outset. She also needed to know that while he liked her kids, he was kind of intimidated by them. Not Katie and Kristen themselves, but the idea of kids. The possibility of messing up with them, of not knowing what to do. And then there was the stability issue. He knew from experience that kids needed stability to grow and thrive. What did he know about stability?

Absolutely nothing.

Annie drove them to a roadside pub on the outskirts of Dillon—a place he'd never been before. "They have great steak sandwiches," she assured him as he held the door open for her.

And beer. They had a great selection of beer on tap. Annie ordered a short and he ordered a tall and they settled back in their chairs to wait for their food. Since there was only one other couple in the pub, their order came quickly. Annie ate half of her sandwich then pushed her plate aside.

"Still nervous?" he asked.

She looked at him in surprise. "Not a bit."

"Then we can consider this a successful outing?"

"I bought a rusty wheelbarrow. Does it get any better than that?"

"Want to do it again?" Trace asked. "Maybe without the wheelbarrow?"

Annie's expression grew serious. "I've been wondering that."

Honest. And direct. Trace ignored the sinking feeling in the pit of his stomach, telling himself he really had no cause to feel disappointed. It wasn't like he had anything to promise but the here and now. When he pictured his life a year from now, there was no question as to where he'd be—on the road, riding bulls, following his dream. He couldn't imagine doing anything else—he felt like he might die a little if he gave up that part of his life.

At some point the bull riding had to stop, but when he imagined himself settling down, living as he was living now…the image didn't gel. He was going stir-crazy at Lex and Grady's place, even with his afternoons spent at the practice pen. He'd find a job that allowed him to be near the action—trucking bulls or working in some other capacity for a stock contractor.

He liked being with Annie, but he had to be true to himself. Which meant coming clean with her. He didn't want her to have any illusions as to how long he'd be around. "While you're making your decision, there's something you should know."

She tilted her head politely, but he could sense the shift in her demeanor.

"No big secret. It's just that I'm not good at staying in one place for long. Never have been."

"Is that a warning?" she asked softly, lifting her beer to her lips and watching him over the top of the glass.

"Full disclosure."

She set the glass back down. "I like honesty."

"It's the way I am," he said simply. "I'm most comfortable when I'm following the circuit."

She looked down at the table, a faint frown creasing her forehead. "While we're disclosing...you do, of course, understand that I have more than just myself to consider when I make decisions."

"I know."

"I had so much fun today." Her hand closed around her napkin and he noticed her emphasis on the past tense. "I like being with you."

"Thank you."

"Ever dated a single mom, Trace?"

He gave his head a shake. "Your girls are the cutest things ever. Funny and fun to be around." His mouth tightened. "They scare me to death."

Annie let out a breath and leaned back in her chair. "I can understand that. I hadn't spent much time around kids, either, until I had them. It was a shock when I discovered that not only were babies a lot of work, there was also a boatload of daily worry and anxiety that went along with all the joys of parenthood."

"You started at the ground level and worked up. I've never been even near the ground level."

Annie's chin dipped down again and Trace reached out to tilt it back up. The disappointed look in her eyes was killing him.

"So," she said slowly. "What we're saying is that even though we are...attracted...to each other, when we look at the realities of our situation...there probably shouldn't be a situation."

"There *can* be a situation," he countered. "But it has to be an eyes-wide-open thing. Like I told you, I won't make promises I can't keep."

"Then I have stuff to think about." She got up from her chair, the legs scraping loudly over the wood floor, and Trace did the same, taking her upper arm in a gentle grip.

"Annie…"

"It's fine, Trace." She sounded as if she meant it. "It's good to be realistic. I think that's why I asked you out—so that we could confront reality. And we have."

She smiled up at him then pushed open the heavy pub door and stepped out into the brisk Montana spring air. Trace followed her to the truck, wishing that he didn't feel like his gut was tying itself into a knot. Honesty was good and they'd been honest. Right?

There was no reason to feel this ridiculous sense of loss after one kiss and a friendly date.

THE DRIVE BACK to Lex's farm wasn't exactly awkward, but it was silent. The elephant in the room had been addressed much earlier than Annie had anticipated. And honestly? She'd thought it would take a couple of dates before her package-deal status and Trace's preferred lifestyle came to the forefront, but it was probably best it had happened this way.

Trace was a guy who followed the road. No matter how well they clicked, Annie would not be following the road. Then there was that matter of Trace being afraid of kids—a deal breaker for sure, except that Annie had watched Trace with her girls and firmly believed that with time, he'd figure out the whole kid thing. He was a natural, but needed the confidence that came with practice. Just her luck to be attracted to a guy who wasn't afraid of a half-ton bull, but was intimidated by a pair of small girls.

Annie dropped Trace off and drove away without experiencing another of his amazing kisses. Better that way. Really, it was. She'd followed her impulse and tested the water and things had ended in the best possible way. No messy breakups when he had to hit the road. No hiding things from her girls.

She was almost to town when her phone rang. Emily.

"Hi, Em. What's up?"

"I think you have a couple sick girls on your hands. They're wilting on the sofa as I speak."

When her girls went down, they went down fast. At least they'd waited until she'd taken care of the other business in her life. "Be right there. Do you mind if I make a quick stop for Popsicles and Jell-O?"

"Not at all."

Annie pulled into the store at the edge of town and stocked up on foods that would be easy for the girls to eat in their current state then hurried on to Emily's house. The girls were ambulatory, but cranky, and Emily helped Annie steer them out to the truck.

"I see you had success at the auction," she said.

"Yes. I was going to have Danielle's dad and Curtis help me unload at the store, but it'll have to wait until tomorrow." Annie watched her girls fasten their seat belts and slump into each other. "Or maybe the next day."

"You have a couple sick babies," Emily agreed.

"They won't be going to school on Monday," Annie said.

"No." Emily hugged herself as the wind gusted. "Let me know when they'll be back."

"Will do. Thanks."

Annie drove her girls home and got them situated on the sofa in front of the television. Even though they would both instantly go to sleep, neither of them liked being in bed when they were sick, and Annie was of the opinion that a sick kid should be in the place where they were most comfortable, and in the case of her girls, that was on the sofa, ignoring the television set.

"What else do you need?" Annie asked as she arranged an afghan over Kristen.

"Nothin'," her daughter muttered as her eyes drifted shut. Katie was already out. And by this time tomorrow, they'd probably be fine. Or so Annie hoped. She hated having them miss too much school, and as it was, they were going to be upset at missing the casting announcement for the elementary play.

Oh, well. They'd get the news, good or bad, on Tuesday or Wednesday.

Annie drifted into the kitchen and sat at the table, laying her head down on her folded arms and closing her eyes. This was what her life was about right now—taking care of her girls. It had been nice going out with Trace, and she appreciated his honesty about his capabilities. In a few years she could date. Right now she was a mom. And she was good at it. She had to be. She was all her girls had.

Chapter Nine

"Wait until you see this one." Jasper Hennessey leaned on the rails while Bill and one of his sons loaded a young bull in the chute.

Trace wasn't yet ready to ride, but his shoulder was regaining its range of motion and he had started strength-building exercises. Another few weeks and he'd be ready to go. He'd already talked to Jasper about practice. Jasper didn't have the caliber of bulls he needed to get a full workout, but he had some animals that Trace could start on. And he didn't plan to do all that much in the practice pen. It would kill him to get injured practicing rather than competing. And he definitely didn't intend to get injured before he rode Brick in December.

The gate opened and a young, riderless bull bucked its way across the arena.

"He has real potential," Trace said. The animal was smaller than the others, but bucked in a serious way. Once he had a little more growth on him, he'd present a decent challenge to the cowboy trying to ride him.

"Good lines. I indulged myself a few years ago and bought three rodeo cows for my breeding program."

"How's that going? Your program?" Because this young bull was definitely of a higher caliber than his older ones.

"Well…let's just say that it started as a sideline and seems to be developing into a full-time business. I barely have time for my farming anymore…which kind of works, because I hate farming. I make Bill do it." Jasper cackled and shifted his attention back to the arena, where Bill herded the young bull toward the gate after his training run.

Raising bucking bulls was one way to stay in the bull-riding business, but it required both property and an infusion of cash. Trace had saved a goodly amount of money—more than the average bull rider—because he'd heeded his mother's warning to put something away for the unexpected. He was a believer in the un-expected, because nothing in his life had turned out as expected—but he hadn't saved enough to buy property and animals. That would involve a loan and settling into a business, staying in one locale, and he didn't know if he wanted to do that.

He didn't know if he *could* do that.

Even now the siren call of the road seemed louder every day. He was antsy and edgy and didn't feel at all himself. Twice last night he'd reached for the phone to call Grady and tell him that he'd need to pull up stakes. Both times he stopped because he was really in an ideal situation—he had a place to work out and there was a practice pen available. He just needed to tamp down this rising sense of panic and get on with preparing for his comeback.

The door opened and Cody walked in, slapping his hat against his leg to shake the water off. He nodded at Trace, who nodded back. The kid had given him a gruff apology the first afternoon Trace had shown up at the practice arena and, after that, things had been okay between them. In fact, during the weeks that they'd hung together, Trace found that he liked the kid. Cody had talent, but too many responsibilities at his family ranch to seriously pursue bull riding. He still practiced diligently and rode in as many events as he could afford to travel to. It was hard not to appreciate his dedication to the sport.

Cody came to lean on the rails next to him, silently watching the last junior bull's training run. "Going to ride today?"

"I wish." Trace was glad to be with his own kind, but he was also envious of his own kind. He wanted to ride in the worst way.

"How much longer until you get your release?"

"I hope to ride in an event at the end of May. I have the entry." He also had an appointment in a week with a doctor in Bozeman who was in communication with his Oklahoma surgeon.

"I see that Grady's doing really well," Cody said. "Did you see the video of his ride last night?"

"Yep." His friend was sitting at number twelve in the standings and was hoping to break into the top ten.

"Seen Annie lately?" Cody continued casually. Almost too casually.

"Once or twice."

Cody shot him a sideways look. "I owe her an apology for what I did in the bar that night. I was drunker than I should have been and pretty much made an ass of myself."

"It happens."

"Are you two, like, seeing each other?"

"Nope." Trace cocked his head to look at the kid sideways. "She's busy being a mom and I'm not going to interfere with that." He gave the kid a stern look. "You probably shouldn't, either."

"Wouldn't matter if I wanted to." Cody kicked the rail in front of him with the toe of his dusty boot, making Trace wonder what had finally woken the kid up to the truth.

"Probably not," he agreed mildly.

Cody gave him a crooked smile. "Some of the guys are going out tonight after practice. New place we need to check out. Want to come?"

"Going to make an ass of yourself?"

"Probably."

Trace grinned. "I wouldn't mind a night out."

"You have fun at your party," Katie said as Annie dropped the girls at Emily's house Saturday morning. Just as Annie had predicted, they'd bounced back fast from their illness last Sunday and only missed one day of school that week.

"Tell Granny happy birthday and that we wish we were there," Kristen added, sounding only a little pouty. To them a birthday party with no kids was no party at all.

"I'll do that," Annie said with a laugh, giving hugs to each girl. "Tomorrow we'll work on the costumes, okay?" The girls had indeed been cast as butterflies, along with thirteen other first- and second-graders. Their relief at not being squirrels had been almost palpable.

"We can draw pictures of what we want to make!" Kristen said.

"As long as it looks like a scarf, great." Annie had found twelve scarves at the local thrift store during her lunch and Granny had donated three more, giving her the basic materials she needed to turn little kids into winged insects. A little glitter, some pipe cleaners and headbands. Yes. She had this.

She had started the day with a burst of energy, even taking time to mop the kitchen floor before loading the girls into the car, but by the time she reached the store, she felt oddly light-headed. The light-headedness became a dull ache as the day progressed, and when it was time to close the store and head to the party at five o'clock, Annie wanted nothing more than to pick up her girls and go home. For Granny's sake she soldiered on.

When they arrived at the brand-new bar and restaurant at the south end of town, the place was already crowded. Danielle pointed to an open door at the opposite side of the room and she and Annie wound their way through the throng of people to the banquet room.

"Glad we didn't start this party at seven, like Mom

wanted," Danielle murmured. Annie nodded. The reason they had it at five o'clock was because due to pregnancy, Danielle conked out around eight every night. "Oh, look! Doesn't Granny look great?"

"She really does. Hope I look that good at eighty."

Dorothy Perry was dressed in an elegant black cocktail dress, and when she caught sight of Danielle and Annie she crossed the room to hug them both.

"Happy birthday, Dorothy," Annie said. "You look wonderful."

"Not a day over seventy-five, right?"

"You look younger than that." Danielle beamed at her grandmother and hugged her again.

"Your mom outdid herself," Annie murmured to Danielle as the guest of honor went to greet two of Danielle's cousins. There were balloons and streamers and a three-layer cake. In the corner a mobile bar was set up so that the guests didn't have to go to the bar proper to get their drinks, which was just as well, because it was getting loud and rowdy out there. Danielle's mother closed the door to their private room after a noisy group settled at a table nearby. Just before the door swung shut, Annie heard Shelly Hensley's distinctive voice rise above the ruckus.

Excellent.

Annie turned down champagne and instead nursed a glass of ice water as she made small talk with Perry friends and family, happy to be part of the tightly knit group, yet also wishing she were at home. Where it was quiet. The party noise was getting to her, making her head throb, and if Dorothy didn't blow out her candles soon, she was going to have to make her excuses and go home while she still could. Her headache wasn't getting worse, though, so she persevered, making small talk until a server set a plate of deviled eggs on the table behind her and her stomach clenched as the smell hit her nostrils.

"I've got to go," she whispered to Danielle.

Instantly her friend was ready to drive her home.

"No," Annie said. "I'm not that far gone, but I want to get the girls and get home before I am."

"Text me when you get home."

Annie smiled, even though it hurt. "I will." She made her way to the door, wincing as she opened it and the noise washed over her. She'd only gone a couple of feet when someone pushed their way in front of her, barring her path.

Shelly. Drunk Shelly. Her least favorite kind of Shelly.

"Well, if it isn't Miss Helpful."

Annie pulled in a breath, barely noticing the crowd around her. She wasn't going to engage Shelly, but she didn't know how she was going to get around her, either. When she stepped sideways, the woman smirked and mirrored her movement.

Annie raised weary eyes and said simply. "Get out of my way, Shelly, or I may just throw up on your shoes."

They were open-toed shoes, high heeled and glittery, and something in Annie's expression must have told Shelly that she wasn't kidding—not one little bit—so the woman quickly stepped aside, an expression of extreme distaste on her face, as several of her cronies laughed.

"Drunk at six o'clock," Shelly said with a curl of her lips.

"Yeah," Annie said as she headed for the door. "What would it be like?"

There was more laughter and then Annie stepped out of the bar and let the heavy door swing shut behind her. Cool air washed over her, making her feel less foggy-headed, but she still needed to get her girls and get home. Fast. Because she had the feeling that whatever this was, it was going to get worse before it got better— just as it had when her girls had caught it.

"You do not look healthy," Emily said a few minutes later as Katie and Kristen put on their coats. "Do you want me to keep the girls for you overnight?"

"No. We'll be fine once we get home." She'd just gone shopping so there was plenty of easy food to eat and all she needed was a little rest.

"If you say so. But give a call if you need anything at all."

Annie nodded and rolled up the window as the girls got into their seats.

"You're sick, Mom?"

"Just a little," Annie said. "I'll take a nap when we get home and you guys can watch TV. Okay?"

"Don't worry," Katie said. "We'll take real good care of you. We'll make Jell-O and everything."

"No," Annie said automatically. "Don't make Jell-O."

Heaven forbid. "I'll be happy with cold orange juice. Or maybe a Popsicle."

"Popsicles helped me," Katie said reassuringly.

In her girls' world, there wasn't much that a Popsicle couldn't cure. She wished things were that easy in her world.

WHEN TRACE, CODY, Bill Hennessey and the rest of the bull-riding crew arrived at the new bar that the boys had wanted to check out, it was ridiculously crowded. And apparently there was a party in the back, too. Trace had just worked his way through the crowd to reach the far end of the bar when he heard a voice that made the muscles in his neck go tight.

Shelly.

She either didn't see him or didn't recognize him, so Trace pulled his hat down a little lower to keep from having another confrontation with the woman.

"I'll take care of the drinks," Cody said. He raised a hand to hail the cute server then made his way through the crowd to intercept her.

"Ah, the vigor of youth," Bill murmured and Trace smiled. A few minutes later Cody was back. "Brianne will get to us as soon as she can." He gave a small laugh. "I guess Shelly confronted Annie a few minutes ago and Annie threatened to throw up on her shoes. Brianne hates Shelly, you know. I guess it was pretty funny."

"Annie's here?" Trace cast a quick look around the crowded room but didn't spot her anywhere.

"Gone. Shelly let her pass. Puke is such an awesome weapon."

Cody seemed to think it was pretty funny, but Trace didn't see the humor—other than the fact that Shelly had apparently backed down. She didn't seem as obnoxious as she had in the Shamrock, but Trace still kept his hat low as he leaned on the bar, listening to the younger guys. Bill leaned silently beside him.

"Getting too old for crowded bars," he finally said.

Trace shook his head. "I must be getting old, too." Although, truthfully, he'd never liked crowded bars. Quiet places where he could enjoy his drink and some decent conversation were more his speed.

"Want to leave this place to the younger crowd?"

"Yeah. I need to go check on a friend."

"I kind of thought you might."

Trace didn't know what to expect when he knocked lightly on Annie's back door twenty minutes later. It was very possible that the girls wouldn't let him in due to the stranger-danger factor, but when they peeked from the side window and saw that it was him, they opened right up.

"Hi, Mr. D'laney," Kristen said. "What are you doing here?"

"I heard your mom wasn't feeling too well and I thought I'd see if you guys were all right."

"We're fine," Katie assured him. "We just got home." She pointed at their coats, which were draped over the backs of the kitchen chairs.

"Is your mom in bed?"

The girls shook their heads in unison. "Uh-uh. Watching TV."

Well, it wasn't as if he could just walk away without telling her he'd stopped by. That would be weird, so he said, "Maybe I could say hello before I go."

Katie took his hand in her much smaller one and led him to the living room where Annie was sound asleep on the sofa, her soft brown hair hiding her face.

"Okay, guys. Your mom isn't feeling too good, so let's let her have a little rest."

"I think she's already asleep," Katie said.

"And we aren't guys," Kristen said. "We're girls."

"Are you sure?"

The girls burst into laughter. "You know we're girls."

"Yeah, I do. I call everyone guys," Trace said in a lower voice so they wouldn't wake Annie, who was indeed passed out. "Even girls." He thought about covering her with the afghan draped over the arm of the easy chair, but didn't want to risk waking her. Instead he turned and headed into the kitchen. As he expected, the girls followed close behind.

Annie's kitchen was neat, like the rest of the house, and full of warmth and color. Now that he had a moment to study the room, he saw that her use of bright paint and cheerful decorations made it easy to overlook the fact that the appliances were ancient or that the windows needed caulking. It looked like Annie was about to tackle that, however, since there were two industrial-sized tubes of caulking on the counter near the toaster.

"Mom said we can't touch those," Kristen said.

"Yeah. She's right." Trace imagined that if the girls managed to get the caulking into the gun, they could create an awesome mess. Grady had told him stories about his nieces, so Trace had an inkling of what he was dealing with here—adventurous girls with lots of energy and ideas. "Have you guys eaten yet?"

"We ate at Emily's," Katie said. "Right after the other kids left with their moms."

"But we're kind of hungry now," Kristen said. "Do you know how to cook? Uncle Grady used to cook when he was here. He cooked lots of stuff in the Crock-Pot."

"He writes us postcards from where he is," Katie announced. "We each get one."

"That's cool," Trace said with a smile, admiring the bounce from Grady cooking to writing postcards.

"Maybe we can cook in the Crock-Pot," Kristen said hopefully.

"I think that might take too long."

"'Sides," Katie said in a authoritative voice, "Mom doesn't let us use plug-in things."

"Then we'll leave the Crock-Pot to your mom. What do you guys like to eat?"

"What we like best is mac and cheese," Katie announced before dashing to the pantry and coming back with two boxes. "One for us and one for you."

Trace hadn't planned on eating there but quickly changed his mind. The longer he stayed, the more downtime Annie would get.

"Do you really want that kind of mac and cheese or the real kind?" Because Trace hated boxed mac and cheese. It'd been one of the few things they could afford to eat when his mom was sick and he'd be quite happy if he never saw an orangish-yellow elbow noodle again in his life.

"The real kind? You can make the real kind?"

"If you have macaroni noodles and cheese, I can."

"We have lots of macaroni."

"We paint it and make necklaces."

"Do you have any unpainted macaroni?"

The girls laughed. "Yes, silly. We have bags and bags." Kristen went to the pantry again and came back with salad macaroni, which Trace could see would make better necklaces than the elbow variety, since the hollow noodles were shorter and barely curved.

"Is that the only kind you have?"

The girls nodded in unison. "Cool. Now we have to be real quiet while your mom sleeps. Katie, can you show me where your pots and pans are? And Kristen, can you find the cheese? Let's see if we have enough."

Oh, yeah. There was enough. Apparently Annie liked cheese. There wasn't much milk, though. He went to the pantry and found a great stash of canned goods, including evaporated milk. Until he'd started hanging out at the McClure Ranch, he'd had no idea that the stuff even existed, but Josie had taught him not only of its existence, but how to use it. On a ranch where the big shopping trip happened once a month, there were certain staples that couldn't be depended on, like fresh milk, so the ranch had had huge stores of canned goods...kind of like Annie did.

With a lot of enthusiastic help, Trace made a white

sauce and boiled the macaroni. He gave each girl a small piece of cheese to grate, while he cut the rest into cubes, which he put in the white sauce to melt. Josie had taught him to take the pan off the heat so that the cheese didn't separate.

He missed Josie and Ernest, the time he'd spent with them, the things he'd learned. He went to the fridge and pulled out the bottle of mustard. The reaction from the girls was instantaneous.

"Ewww!"

"No mustard!" Kristen made another horrified face.

"Just a teaspoon."

Katie's mouth flattened.

"It's the secret ingredient in all good mac and cheese." Two little noses wrinkled. "The thing is, when you mix mustard with cheese, it tastes way different than when it's on a hot dog." The girls gave him another dubious look and he put the mustard back in the fridge. It was their dinner, after all. So what if the mac and cheese was minus the zing of mustard?

"What do we do with *our* cheese?"

"We put that on top."

The girls sprinkled the cheese and helped spread it evenly over the macaroni that Trace had poured into a cake pan. He put it in the oven and set the timer.

"Now what?"

Well, he certainly couldn't leave the macaroni cooking and go home. "What do you guys—girls—usually do while waiting for supper to cook?"

"We do our schoolwork."

"Or watch TV."

"Or play on the computer."

"Or play dolls."

Katie's face brightened. "Yeah. You can be the boy dolls!"

"I…"

But Kristen was already on her way out of the room, Katie close behind her. A moment later they came back carrying a box of dolls and small clothing.

Trace pushed the hair back from his forehead. This was foreign territory.

Katie set three fashion dolls in various states of dress on the table then looked up at Trace. "Who do you want to be?"

"Uh…where's that guy doll you were talking about?"

Kristen dug into the bin and pulled out two identical boy dolls—one wearing striped pajamas and the other wearing jeans and a white shirt with an aluminum foil buckle on his small belt. "This is Tyler and this is Jess. They're twins. Like us."

Trace knew Tyler and Jess Hayward, the bull-riding twins. He wondered if they knew they had tiny doppelgangers.

"We don't have many boy clothes," Katie said.

"And they don't fit in the girl jeans, so Tyler has to wear his pajamas."

"Or his beach shorts." Katie pulled out a pair of flowered swim trunks.

Trace picked up Tyler. "So, what's my job?"

"We have to get the horses and then we play rodeo."

Not what he'd been expecting.

"Uncle Grady got us a bull, too, so Tyler and Jess can ride the bull."

"In his pajamas?" Trace asked.

"Well, he has to wear something," Katie remarked in a grown-up tone as she headed out of the room. She reappeared a few minutes later with a crate of horses and, sure enough, there was a Brahma bull in with the plastic model horses.

"I'll get the cans," Kristen said.

"Cans?"

"For barrel racing," Katie said as if he was slow on the uptake.

And so Trace got down on the floor and played rodeo with the girls. Tyler did very well riding the bull, but Jess got tossed off and landed in the sink of soapy water with a big splash, much to the girls' delight.

"Mom never lets us do that."

"Mom…" He almost said "doesn't need to know" before he realized that was not a very wise thing to say to two impressionable seven-year-olds. "Mom knows best," he amended. He got to his feet and fished Jess out of the sink and left him to dry on the drain rack before sitting back down again. Out of curiosity, he asked, "Do you guys ever play anything but rodeo?"

"Sometimes we play school and sometimes we play going-on-a-date, but mostly we play rodeo."

"You can go on a date *to* a rodeo," Kristen announced. "That's where Uncle Grady and Lex went on their first date."

"We went, too!" Katie added.

"That must have been some first date."

"It was," Kristen said, suddenly solemn. "Lex got scared and sad because her dad died at a rodeo, but Uncle Grady helped her get not afraid."

"And now they're getting married," Katie interjected.

"We're flower girls!"

Trace fought a smile and then the timer dinged. "Dinner is done," he said, getting to his feet. Why don't you two put this stuff back in the box before we eat? I'll set the table."

And then he'd check on Annie, something he'd wanted to do ever since he started playing the rodeo game.

Chapter Ten

Annie paused briefly outside the kitchen door, a hand on the wall to keep her balance because she was still very light-headed. Trace hadn't seen her as he pushed himself up from where he'd been sitting on the floor, playing rodeo with the girls. He'd made dinner. Annie didn't quite know what to make of that. Actually she was too tired and weak to try to make something of it.

She headed to the bathroom where she looked longingly at her robe hanging on the door before washing her hands and walking back down the hall. The girls were setting the table in the kitchen and Trace was waiting for her in the living room.

"Feeling any better?"

"I'd be lying if I said yes." Her voice was hoarse. Barely a croak. Whatever this bug was, it worked fast. "You don't need to stay, you know."

"Yeah. I know." He gave her a patient look. "Here's the deal…this is very much like you scraping me up out of the parking lot and forcing me to go home with you even when I didn't want to."

"Is it?" she asked, somehow managing to cock one eyebrow.

"Yeah. It is. You're at a disadvantage and I'm here to help, even though you don't think you need help."

"If you say so." She closed her eyes, felt the room start to spin.

"As soon as the girls eat and we wash the dishes, I'm leaving. I'll leave now if you want, but I'll feel better knowing that the girls are fed."

"What are they eating?" She didn't bother to open her eyes.

"Mac and cheese. The homemade kind."

Now her eyes opened. "Homemade macaroni and cheese?"

"One of my specialties."

"I wish I felt better. I love homemade macaroni." She reached for the afghan folded over the arm of the sofa and dragged it up over her, clutching it with her fist just below her chin. "I haven't been sick in years. I hate it."

"I know," he said gently before turning and leaving the room, the old floorboards squeaking under his boots. A few minutes later the girls came into the room, but they didn't climb up on the sofa to snuggle next to her as they usually did. Probably for the best.

"We're checking on you," Katie announced.

"Before we eat. Trace made macaroni."

"You should call him Mr. Delaney," Annie murmured.

"He played rodeo with us, Mom. He said to call him Trace."

"Well, if he played rodeo, that changes things. You should eat before it gets cold."

"We'll save you some," Katie promised. "It smells really good."

"And don't worry," Kristen added. "There's no mustard."

No mustard. Annie let her head slump sideways. She loved mustard.

"I'm going now." Annie jerked upright at the sound of Trace's voice and she realized that she'd fallen asleep. He came closer and held out her phone. "Would you let me put my number in it? Just in case?"

Annie didn't argue. She unlocked the phone and handed it back. A few seconds later he put it on the end table beside her. "Feel better, Annie. Call if you need me."

ANNIE MADE IT a point to call Trace the next day to tell him she didn't need him. She was feeling better. Not that much better, but enough better that she could cook for the girls and get around on her own. Not fall asleep every time she sat down. And since it was Sunday, she had a full day to recover.

"I hope you don't catch this," she said. Because she wouldn't have wished this on anyone, except for maybe Shelly.

"I doubt I will. I have a constitution of steel. All the travel."

"Grady's the same way." An awkward silence followed, the kind that came when something needed to be said and wasn't, which was ridiculous because

Annie had nothing else to say except for thank you, and she'd done that.

"I'll see you around, Annie."

"Yeah. Thanks again."

She hung up her phone and leaned back against the sofa cushions. Would he see her around? She didn't see how, unless they ran into each other by accident.

The phone rang in her hand, startling her. Danielle.

"How are you feeling?" Danielle asked.

"Better, but I may not make it in tomorrow."

"That works, because you're not allowed to come in tomorrow."

"Thank you." Annie felt a swell of relief. She hated missing work, so permission to recover at home was gold.

"We can't risk you throwing up on anyone's shoes," Danielle added on an amused note.

Annie pressed her hand to her aching head. "You heard?" Which was a dumb question. Of course she'd heard.

"Granny's disappointed that she missed witnessing the incident."

"Don't make me laugh. It makes my head ache."

"I'll see you on Tuesday if you're better. *If* you're better," she repeated.

"I'll be better," Annie promised.

DANIELLE'S HUSBAND, CURTIS, drove to Annie's house on Monday morning and picked up the girls for school. Annie hated being a burden on anyone, but she was also extremely grateful to have two such good friends.

"More good practice," she said as the girls raced to Curtis's car.

"Danielle felt the baby move," Curtis said excitedly. "And on a different note, Danielle says that you are to stay off your feet and not use this time to catch up on household chores."

"As if," Annie murmured. Although, she had thought it would be a good day for laundry.

"I'm supposed to get a promise," Curtis said.

"Promise. And thank you."

Annie was very glad she'd made the promise. The laundry was stacked up, but she felt weak and because of the promise, didn't push things. She slept. And slept. And slept. The sound of the back door opening finally woke her, but by the time she got into the kitchen, the girls were already taking off their coats and dumping their school papers on the table.

When Katie saw her, she went to the door and yelled out, "She's awake!"

Annie went to the window in time to see Curtis raise a hand to Katie and then roll up his car window and put the car in motion.

"He didn't want to bother you, but wanted to know if you were better," Kristen explained.

"That was nice of him. Did you have a good day?"

The twins started chattering about their day as Annie headed back to the sofa, making appropriate remarks as they went. She felt better, but was still a touch light-headed. She settled back into her nest and Kristen pulled the afghan up over her.

"You go to sleep, Mama. We'll have cereal for supper."

Not a bad idea. "Put milk and bananas on it," she said. "And eat some peanut butter crackers." Because they needed protein. "Clean up after yourselves…"

"Do you want us to bring you some crackers?"

"Not yet."

"Mr. D'laney's here," Kristen called from the kitchen just as Annie had turned on the television.

She let her head fall back against the pillow. Really? What part of "I don't need you" had he not fully understood? And why did a small part of her jump for joy upon hearing that he was there?

Because she was simply too damned weak where he was concerned, that was why. Well, she was about to get tough. Tamping down a feeling of guilt because he had fed the girls the night before, she got to her feet and started to the kitchen, but she stopped just outside the door when she heard Trace say, "You don't need to bother your mom. I made extra stew today. It's heavy, so let's just put it on the stove, okay?"

"Does it need cooked some more?" Kristen asked hopefully.

"No. Uh…don't cook it. Don't turn on any burners. Do you understand? *No* burners."

"Are you riding bulls now?" Katie asked as if he hadn't said a word about burners.

"Mom said that you're too hurt to ride bulls," Kristen added.

"I'll ride bulls really soon," he said. "Did you understand about the burners?"

"Then you gotta leave, right?" Annie closed her eyes, wondering how they knew that.

"That's right."

"My mom is going to miss you." Annie's eyes shot open and the next thing she knew she was stumbling into the kitchen, pushing her tangled hair back from her forehead.

"Hi," she said as she came to a stop next to the table, taking note first of the Dutch oven sitting on her stove and then the man who'd brought it.

"Hi," Trace echoed, running his gaze over her as if making certain she was all there. Annie could only imagine how she looked, with her hair all wild, wearing her favorite oversize red flannel pajamas. "I didn't want to bother you. I just wanted to make sure you were all right."

"And you made us stew."

He moved a couple of steps closer to her. "I like to cook, Annie." He tilted his head at her girls. "Rumor has it that these guys—girls—like to eat, and you're clearly under the weather."

"There's no turnips in the stew, right, Trace?" Katie asked.

"No turnips, no mustard," he said, holding Annie's gaze.

Her mouth twitched. "I think you know exactly what my thoughts are right now."

"I have a good idea," he said lowly. "But rest assured, I'm not pushing my way into your..." His voice trailed off as he suddenly realized that the girls were following the conversation closely, their faces turning back and forth between the two of them as they spoke. *"L-I-F-E."* He finished by spelling the word.

"Lll…iiii…" Katie started sounding out the letters.

"Fuh," Kristen finished triumphantly. "Life!"

Trace's eyes widened in surprise and Annie suddenly felt like laughing. "Yes, sweetie. Life. Very good."

"We had that word on my last spelling test!" Kristen said smugly.

"Mrs. Lawrence will give us that word *this* week," Katie assured her sister. "And we've had words that *your* class hasn't had yet."

"Which ones?" Kristen demanded.

"Why don't you girls go sort the scarves?" Annie asked.

Two pairs of green eyes swung her way. "But you said we had to wait to touch them."

"You can touch them now. They're in the box next to my bed."

The girls raced out of the room, leaving Annie and Trace very much alone. Almost too alone. And Trace had a decided advantage, being fully clothed with his hair combed. In the makeup department they were dead even. Neither of them wore any.

"Bright girls," Trace muttered.

"What can I say?" Annie murmured back.

His eyes narrowed a little, the dark lashes making the green parts of his hazel eyes appear even greener. "Annie…I'm kind of wondering where we are here."

"What do you mean?"

He gestured at a chair. "You want to sit down?"

"Before I fall down, you mean?"

"You do look a little wobbly."

Annie sat. Truth be told, she felt wobbly.

"What I meant was, what did we decide on that first date?"

"The only date."

"That's the one."

Annie drew in a breath and resisted the impulse to lay her head down on the table, close her eyes. Disappear. She wasn't 100 percent and maybe this wasn't the best time to be discussing this matter. Maybe Trace was aware of that and taking advantage of her weakness.

For what end?

She couldn't think of one.

She shrugged and focused on the cheerful cherry motif placemat in front of her. "We agreed that you're a traveling guy and that you're not used to kids and that I'm not a traveler and my kids are my life." Silence followed her words. She raised her gaze from the cherries and found him studying her with an unreadable expression. "Right?" she asked, feeling oddly uncertain.

"Yeah. That sums it up. But we didn't decide that we disliked each other or anything."

"No. We did not."

"Then why act that way?"

"I'm not acting that way. I just don't see any good coming out of us hanging out together."

"And what kind of bad can you see coming out of it, Annie?"

"The girls will get attached."

"They just told me very matter-of-factly, and without one trace of regret, that they know I'm leaving." He hooked a thumb in his belt. "And that you'd miss me."

Meaning she was the one who was getting attached. Annie's chin tilted up, but she found she had nothing to say. "I will miss you," she finally said. "But *I* can't afford to get attached to you."

"So we won't see each other anymore?"

"That was the plan, but you keep bringing food," she muttered.

He took the chair opposite hers and, after checking quickly to make certain no small interested faces were in view, reached out to take her hand in his.

"I'm contagious," she murmured, but she allowed him to curl his fingers around hers.

"I know," he said in a way that made it obvious that he wasn't talking germs and disease. "Annie—"

"What I'm afraid of," she blurted, cutting him off, "is not being able to resist temptation." She met his gaze, suddenly feeling a whole lot braver now that the truth was out. "Because you're tempting."

His eyebrows rose, but he didn't seem displeased by her admission. "So are you."

"Can you see where that might lead to trouble?"

"I can," he said slowly. "But I think we can head it off."

Annie frowned at him. "What are you asking for, Trace?" The sounds of laughter drifted into the kitchen from the direction of Annie's bedroom and she was glad that the girls were occupied with the scarves. Although they could flutter in at any moment, so she wanted to settle as much of this unsettling business as possible before that happened.

"I guess I'm just asking you not to shut me out, Annie. Circumstances aren't right at this point in time, but…" He shrugged.

"Someday you won't be riding bulls and someday my girls will be grown?"

Another shrug, but he held her eyes, his expression serious.

She glanced down at the cherries again before once again meeting his gaze. "Even if you don't ride bulls, could you settle for such a different life, a life like mine?" Because ultimately, that would be what she was looking for.

"I guess that's what I need to find out."

"I won't be your guinea pig in that regard, Trace. Not while the girls are young." He started to speak, but she cut him off, weary of a battle with herself she wasn't going to win. "But…I'll be your friend."

"My friend."

"Without benefits. A friend. Period."

"All right."

"With no talk of being tempting or tempted." Because setting strong boundaries was the only way she could spend time with this man—and, yes, she still wanted to spend time with him. The thought of never seeing him again killed her. Someday he *would* stop bull riding, and someday her girls wouldn't need her as much as they did now. And maybe then…

Trace's hand tightened over hers, and then he pulled his fingers away as if sealing the no-temptation deal.

"I can accept that. I want to be your friend, if that's all I can be." The *now* went unspoken, but Annie's breath still caught a little.

"What is it you want out of this…friendship?" Annie asked. Because she had to.

"I just want you to feel free to call on me if you need help. Maybe we can share a few meals. Ride in the mountains again. Just do some stuff before I leave."

"When will that be?" Because the last time she'd talked to Grady, he fully intended to stay on the road until the end of May, driving to as many events as distance allowed and flying to the others. Lex was talking about starting a family and she wanted to see all of the country she could before settling down.

"I have an event at the end of May. I won't have a lot of practice rides before then, but I figure kinetic memory will see me through."

"You'll be healed?"

"I'm not pushing things."

"You should share that helpful hint with my brother."

Trace smiled a little. "Wouldn't do any good." He shifted his weight in the chair. "I'm still a little shaky on dealing with kids, but I like spending time with your family, Annie. I'm glad I can still do that."

Annie propped an elbow on the table and rested her forehead in her hand. She was starting to fade. "You don't find kids as intimidating as before?"

"I'm feeling my way along. I'd like to be more… confident, I guess. I never know if they get what I'm saying, you know?"

"I know." That was simply a matter of practice, of

learning to read signs and checking for understanding. Things that were second nature to her now that hadn't been before she'd had kids. "Anything else I should know?"

"I have no idea what I'm doing here, Annie, but I don't like kicking around that big old farmhouse while wondering what you and the kids are doing."

Hell of an admission, that.

"So you make us stew."

"So I make you stew."

Annie's lips tilted up for the first time since Trace had walked in the door. "You think the friendship thing will work?"

"I want to try."

"In that case, how do you feel about butterfly costumes and rusty wheelbarrows?"

Chapter Eleven

Glitter, as it turned out, was very tricky stuff. When he stopped by the next evening after visiting the practice pen, Annie was back on her feet and experimenting with pieces of lightweight fabric and glitter paint trying to make sparkly wings. Unfortunately, the sparkly gunk weighted down the scarves to the point that they didn't flutter. Instead they stuck to the twins as they twirled and swirled in circles in the living room.

"Do they have to be glittery?" Trace asked, earning himself stern looks from the girls. "Sorry," he muttered.

"I think Trace is right," Annie said. "I know you wanted glitter, but you also want to be fluttery like a real butterfly, right?"

"Yes," Katie said.

"But we want to sparkle, too," Kristen added in a stubborn voice.

"Here's the thing," Annie said, reaching out to take each of the girls' hands in her own and pulling them down next to her. "Sometimes in life you can't have two things that you want. They cancel each other out.

You have to choose one or the other. So—" she looked at each twin in turn "—do you want to sparkle? Or do you want to flutter?"

"Can we think about it?"

Annie gave a solemn nod and Trace wondered if Annie was aware of the irony of the lecture she'd just given. He wasn't concerned with sparkling or fluttering, but he did seem to want two things that canceled each other out.

"Does this excuse me from butterfly duty?" Trace asked.

Annie gave him a wry look. "The glitter part. I still have to make fifteen antennae." She waved her hand at a box of hair bands, pipe cleaners and puff balls."

Trace's eyebrows lifted. This parent business had some interesting side roads. "Can you dilute that glitter paint with water or something and brush it on?"

"Hey," Annie said. "Good idea." She picked up the paint and hauled it toward the bathroom. "My kitchen faucet conked out. Has a leak, so I'm not using it."

"When are you fixing it?"

"Tomorrow. But the dishwasher works, so I'm in decent shape."

"Old houses are an adventure, aren't they?" He liked this. The give and take of conversation with no agenda. Just talking and being. He'd never done a lot of this before, except with Ernest and Josie, but he'd always felt as if they were always on the lookout for a teachable moment. This was just talk.

"Oh, so you know about old houses?" Annie came out of the bathroom with a small paper cup of water and then walked into the kitchen where her fabric scraps were still on the table. She squeezed some glitter glue onto a small plate, then slowly stirred water into it.

"Lived in a few," he said, sitting at the table next to her. Annie nodded at the brush just out of reach and he handed it to her, taking care not to brush his fingers against hers. She'd said no touching, no being tempted. He could control no touching.

"This might work." She brushed the glitter over the cloth then spread it out to dry.

"And then the girls will have two things that should have canceled each other out but didn't."

Annie looked up to frown at him, but she made no reply. The timer dinged and she pushed out of her chair.

"By the way, thanks so much for the stew." Annie pulled a pan of lasagna out of the oven and set it on top of a metal rack. "I took the last of it for lunch today. It certainly beat a sandwich." And she was certainly guiding the conversation back to safe topics. She went to the fridge to take out a salad, which she put on the counter. "Tell me about your old houses."

Trace glanced down at the table briefly, then decided to give her the full story. Why not?

"While she was still alive, we lived in Reno. Mom worked in a casino until she got too sick to go to work. The old houses I lived in weren't very nice. The better ones were cut up into apartments. The other ones… like I said, not so nice." But at least he hadn't been on the streets, like some kids he knew.

A sympathetic expression formed on Annie's face.

"And when your mom died, you went to live with your dad?"

"Yeah. He passed away just a few months ago. Right before my surgery."

"I'm sorry to hear that."

"Thank you. But honestly? We weren't that close."

"I kind of guess that when you called him a distant relative."

"It wasn't an easy situation. He and my mom hadn't been together that long when she got pregnant with me." He drummed his fingers, then stopped. "And we never were able to work through the awkwardness. I was actually closer to his neighbor, Ernest. He's the guy who got me into bull riding. My dad just wanted me gone. I didn't fit into his life. He had legitimate sons to focus on."

"Trace…that's horrible."

"I've made my peace."

"Have you?"

He stood and crossed to where she stood. He wanted to put his hands on her shoulders, but he'd promised no touching. "Yeah. I have." She studied him for a long moment, a slight frown marring her smooth forehead. "It was either make peace or go crazy."

"Yet this is all tied to your bull-riding career, isn't it?"

"It's made me who I am today. And I don't mean that in a bad way." Because somehow saying those words made him feel like he was admitting to being damaged. He wasn't. He'd gone through some hell in his life, but he'd learned to deal. He'd found an outlet for his frustrations in bull riding and for that he'd be forever grateful.

"How about your parents?" he asked. "Where are they?" He and Grady had never discussed their families, probably because Trace didn't have one.

Annie turned back to the cupboards and pulled out a drawer. Silverware rattled and she chose the pieces she wanted. "Dad was a trucker. He passed away while we were in high school. My mom remarried to a really nice guy, but unfortunately got uterine cancer and they didn't find it until it was too late."

"That sucks."

"I was lost for a while. Hooked up with Wes—" she gave him a sideways look "—the twins' father, for security. It didn't work out to be all that secure. I got pregnant. He got scared." She brushed her hair back. "I'm glad. I'd rather raise the girls alone. He turned out to be kind of a weak character."

"Did he make promises he didn't keep?"

It took Annie a moment to say, "Yes. He did. Big ones."

That was what Trace was trying so very hard not to do. He wanted to spend time with Annie while he could, but he didn't want to make promises he couldn't keep.

It kind of felt like he wanted the impossible.

THE NEXT DAY when Trace got to practice, the life-size Hayward twins, Jess and Tyler, were there. Trace knew Tyler from the circuit, but he'd never met Jess, who only rode part-time.

"Good to see you," Tyler said, clapping Trace on the arm.

"You, too," Trace said, idly wondering what Tyler would think about his tiny counterpart wearing pajamas, while his twin wore the championship buckle. In real life, Tyler wore the buckle. Trace indicated Tyler's knee brace with a jerk of his chin. "Are you out for a while?"

"Just home to visit the family. Hitting the road tomorrow."

"I'm the family." Jess offered a hand.

"I feel like I know you," Trace said. The twins were truly identical, except for the small scar on Tyler's chin.

"I get that a lot." Jess smiled easily and Trace fell into step with him as the group ambled toward the arena.

"I hear you're the responsible one. Full-time job and all that."

Jess quirked up a corner of his mouth. "Pretty much, although my full-time job doesn't pay what Ty's been bringing home lately." He shook his head. "But I can't afford to quit yet."

"It's a big decision." And if Jess waited too long, he'd be too old to ride. But every guy had to make his own career decisions and apparently Jess was all about playing it safe, while Tyler took the chances. Just the opposite of the way they behaved in Katie and Kristen's rodeo game—which Trace was fairly certain he'd be playing that evening.

"When do you go back?" Jess asked.

"Soon. I should get my release soon." And then he'd

make up for lost time. He was so looking forward to reestablishing himself.

When practice started, Jess rode and Tyler watched, studying his brother's performance with a critical eye, although there wasn't much to criticize. Jess was a natural talent, just like his brother.

"I wish I could get him out on the road with me," Tyler muttered.

Trace gave a nod. "He's good."

"And cautious." Tyler glanced over at Trace. "Not in the arena. In life."

"And you're not."

It was a statement not a question and Tyler gave Trace a what-can-I-say shrug.

Indeed. What could he say? Trace liked his matter-of-fact acceptance of himself. He felt the same way. He was what he was and did what he had to do. And he was up front about it, which was why he felt comfortable spending time with Annie. Being her friend. And if sometimes his thoughts strayed in a direction that was more than friendly...well, he was leaving soon and she never needed to know.

ANNIE HAD BARELY gotten home when Trace stopped by her house after spending a couple of hours at Hennessey's. He offered to help her prep for supper, but she declined, so he settled in for a rousing game of rodeo while Annie tended to other business around the house. The girls very much wanted him to let Jess get bucked off into the sink again, but Trace whispered to them that it was never a good idea to upset the cook—in this case their mother, who'd worked all day and was still on her feet. He wanted to help her cook, but realized that entertaining the girls was as big a help as peeling potatoes would have been. It was also a lot more fun.

"Felicity and the dogs are going to be jealous that I'm eating here with you guys instead of with them," Trace teased.

"They could come here."

"And knock all the rodeo stuff around?" Trace asked.

Kristen gave a thoughtful nod. "Lex calls Dave a terror."

Dave the terrier was a terror. A lovable one, but a terror all the same.

"You know what?" Katie asked as she put her doll onto the plastic horse in preparation for a barrel run around two cans of spinach and a can of creamed corn.

"What?" Trace asked.

"Well," she said, pressing her lips together momentarily. "When Uncle Grady gets back, we can all play rodeo. He can be Jess and you can be Tyler and we'll be us."

"That sounds great," he said as Annie glanced over at him.

"You know that Uncle Grady cheats at rodeo," Kristen said to Katie as if Grady were a lost cause. "Every. Single. Time."

"How does he cheat?" Trace asked.

"He loses the bull right after his guy rides it. It escapes and we don't find it until it's time to put the stuff away."

"So his guy wins every time?"

"That's why Jess has a buckle and Tyler wears pajamas."

"I see." The championship buckle and the loser pajamas. He might have to pass that idea along.

Annie turned back to her cooking and Trace briefly let his gaze slide down to her shapely backside.

"Are you ready?" Katie demanded.

He got his phone out and set it on the floor and then brought up the timer. "Totally ready."

After Katie's stellar barrel run, Kristen had hers. Then Tyler and Jess both rode the bull and Trace made certain Tyler won so that he didn't have to always wear the pajamas.

"Now we have to make him a buckle," Katie said.

"Can't he wear this one?" Trace asked, pointing at the aluminum foil buckle on Jess's small belt.

Kristen cocked her head at him. "Do you share your buckles?"

"Uh...no."

She shrugged as if the matter was settled and then Annie told them it was time to set the table. The rodeo was over.

TRACE DIDN'T STOP by every night, and he always called before he arrived, to make certain he wasn't encroaching on family time, but the truth of the matter was that the more time he spent at Annie's house, the more he kind of felt like family. He helped her with butterfly costumes one night, and tackled the cranky water main the next so that she could install her new faucet. After that she didn't see him for a few days, then he'd invited the girls to ride and they'd had a nice outing before the rain drove them back to Lex's house. Once there, they'd made instant hot chocolate and sat around Lex's propane fireplace, drinking cocoa and then watching the girls show off the steps to the butterfly dance they were learning. It was three weeks until the big play—an eternity! The classes only got to practice a few minutes a day now, but later they'd get a dress 'hearsal and everything!

Trace walked Annie and the girls to their car after the rain had stopped and while the girls jumped puddles, he and Annie sauntered to a stop near her car. And Annie wanted to touch Trace. Wanted to reach out and run her hand over his tightly muscled arms, let the other hand smooth over his hard abdomen. It must have shown in her face because when she met Trace's eyes, she saw her needs reflected there.

This was the part where she needed to stand strong. If she didn't, it would screw everything up. Since her accidental pregnancy, she'd been nuts about controlling her life, but this was a case where she couldn't control her life, but she could control her actions. And even though she'd never, ever admit it—at this point, anyway—and despite everything she'd told Trace when they'd hammered out this friendship-only deal while sitting at her kitchen table—she felt a small glimmer of hope. Hope that maybe this friendship might grow into something more. Eventually. But it could only do that if Trace came to the conclusion that he could stay in one place. That he didn't need the road as much as he might need some stability.

He had to realize that on his own and until he did, she wasn't going to let things get out of hand.

Which, unfortunately meant not touching or being touched.

It was killing her.

"Paint the wheelbarrow tomorrow?" Trace asked, but from the way he was looking at her, she didn't think wheelbarrows were foremost in his mind.

"Yeah. We still on for this weekend?"

He'd promised to help her pick up a large oak table from a nearby ranch—a table she'd found on the want-ad board at the grocery store, which was going to her house, not the boutique.

"We're on. I'll have to get back for practice, though." He smiled a little. "First ride...if the doctor agrees. I see him Friday."

A tiny stone dropped into Annie's pool of satisfaction. "First ride. Can't miss that."

As a bull rider's sister, she knew how important that first ride after an injury was. The rider needed to know that he was back where he'd been before getting hurt, and if he wasn't back, he needed to gauge how far he needed to go to get there—and beyond.

"You could come watch, you know."

Annie shook her head. This was his deal, not hers. The deal that was going to take him away from her. "Maybe another time."

He started to reach for her then dropped his hand. "Yeah. Maybe another time."

ANNIE AND TRACE had just loaded the oak table and covered it with a tarp when the first fat drops of rain hit his denim jacket and he looked up at the charcoal-gray sky. "We better hit the road."

If he hadn't wasted time driving to the Bozeman Clinic for his release yesterday, only to be told that the doctor had been called to an emergency surgery, they could have picked up the table yesterday, when it had been dry. As it was, they were racing the weather and he had to wait another week to get his release. That didn't sit well with him, but there wasn't a lot he could do—about the release or the weather.

"I'd hoped for another hour," Annie said as she headed for her side of the truck, the rain pattering on the hood and bouncing in the mud before Trace opened his door. Almost as soon as he got inside, the sky opened and the rain poured down.

Getting the table had been a do-or-die thing. The rancher had sold out and was moving to the far side of the state. He didn't want to wait for the weather to clear, so Trace and Annie had packed the tarp and hoped for the best.

The best didn't happen. The rain kept pounding and Annie kept sending worried looks out the rear window of the truck. They'd set the table legs on planks, just in case they didn't beat the rain, and the tarp was secured with more bungee cords than they'd really needed. Annie really wanted this table and Trace was going to see that she got it.

The road they traveled was not well graveled and the rain had made it slick in places, so he drove carefully.

The clouds hung low, making it difficult to see even though the wipers were on high, and Trace slowed even further, apparently too slow for the truck that came up behind him. The big diesel was hauling a trailer and it roared past them, splattering mud across the windshield. Trace's mouth tightened as the wipers smeared the muck into a thin layer before the rain rinsed the windshield clean. Idiot.

"Do you know that guy?" Trace asked.

"The rig's familiar, but I can't put a name on it," Annie said.

"He may not make it home if he continues at that speed."

Annie did not disagree with him. She looked at her table again then focused straight ahead while he slowed to negotiate a series of curves. Five more miles and they'd hit the main road, twenty more miles and he'd be able to get Annie's table out of the rain and she could stop worrying about it.

He rounded another corner then stood on the brakes. "Son of a—" His teeth gritted as the truck fishtailed then came to a stop inches away from the back of an aluminum trailer that was half-in half-out of the ditch, jackknifed and blocking the road, but still attached to the diesel truck tilted at a crazy angle in the ditch. The same diesel that had passed him five minutes before.

Trace muttered a curse, then glanced over at Annie who had one hand braced against the dash. "Are you okay?"

"Yes. I'll head back to warn traffic." Annie yanked a raincoat out of her tote bag, but only had one arm in the sleeve when she opened the door and stepped out into the rain.

Trace pulled his hat down lower as he pushed his door open and got out onto the slippery road. Cattle bawled as he passed the trailer on his way to the truck, and he could hear their feet scrambling for purchase in the drunkenly tilted trailer.

When he reached the cab, the driver was just righting himself from where he'd been slumped against the steering wheel. He blinked at Trace through the rain-smeared window and Trace yanked the door open.

"Don't move."

The guy ignored him and tried to shove his way out of the truck, then let out a low moan of pain and slumped back into his seat. Ribs, probably. And he had a giant goose egg on his forehead. Trace wondered briefly why the air bags hadn't deployed, then realized that the truck was too old to have them.

"Sit tight."

"My cattle."

"I'll get your cattle."

Trace heard the sounds of an engine through the rain and turned to see a truck slowly round the curve. Annie must have been able to flag them down and warn them.

"We need to get this guy to a hospital," Trace said when the passenger window lowered. "Can you call 911?"

"No signal here," the woman said brusquely as she climbed out of the truck and made her way around the front.

"I don't need to go to the hospital," the man in the truck muttered.

"You're going to the hospital, Gordon."

"You know him?" Trace asked.

"Yes," she said grimly. "I know Lead Foot."

A car inched its way around the corner and stopped behind the truck. "Gordon?" the man said when he got out.

Trace stepped back and let Gordon's friends load him into the car, which took off for the hospital, despite the man's weak protests.

Annie came trotting up then, her hair hanging in wet hanks despite her hood. "I have a person parked on the other side of the corner." She grimaced as the cows thrashed.

"Yeah, we got to get them out of there."

The woman, who introduced herself as Sadie, followed Trace and Annie to the trailer, where Trace reefed on the door until he managed to get it unlatched. The four steers were wild-eyed as they climbed over one another in their desperation to get out of the tilted trailer. Moments later they were galloping off into the fog.

"It may be a while until Gordon sees his steers again," Trace commented. "Kind of amazing that only one of them is limping."

"Can't hurt a Corriente," Sadie muttered.

Half an hour later, with the help of Sadie and another passerby, they had the truck dug out and had managed to tow it and the trailer back onto the road. Sadie got behind the wheel once it was determined that the axel was all right and one of the other two guys who'd stopped to help got into Sadie's truck. They drove away, one after the other, leaving Trace and Annie standing in the rain, watching the taillights disappear.

"I'm too cold to shiver," Annie said.

Trace turned to her and noted that she was completely muddy on one side, despite the rain. "I fell down a while back," she said in answer to his unspoken question. "And you don't look much better."

Indeed he was muddy.

Annie pushed the wet hair away from her cheek, but a few stubborn strands clung to her pale skin. "I'll give you this—you know how to show a girl an interesting time."

"It's a mad skill," Trace said as they started slogging their way down the muddy road.

"Uh-huh."

He opened the door for her and she climbed inside. The heater had been running the entire time they'd worked to get the truck and trailer out of the ditch and Annie gave a shudder as the warm air hit her.

"I feel like taking my wet clothing off and basking in warmth."

"I won't stop you," Trace said as he reached for his seat belt. He stilled with his hand on the buckle and met her gaze. "Well, I wouldn't."

Annie held his gaze for what seemed like forever, looking tempted and conflicted. Then she eased across the seat, took his face in both her cold palms and brought her mouth to his. The first touch was soft, yet electric. Annie's hands may have been cold, but her lips were warm and luscious, and Trace was instantly hard. And then the kiss deepened. Trace put his arms around her and hauled her closer, cursing the interference of the steering wheel.

His hands slid down to span the curve of her waist when a horn honk startled them both. Annie jumped and Trace turned to clear the condensation off the side window with his sleeve. The white crew cab Ford had slowed to a crawl as it passed them. The driver honked again and waved, making a face at Trace. Typical bull rider.

"Don Maguire," Annie said putting a little more space between them. "One of Grady's friends."

"I know him from Hennessey's." And despite the condensation on the windows, it was pretty obvious what he and Annie had been doing, which was why Donnie was honking and waving like an idiot. Trace slumped back in his seat, telling himself this was probably a good thing because it brought him crashing back to earth. What was he doing here?

He turned to see Annie studying him, a slight tilt to her luscious mouth as she waited for him to decide the next move. She'd already made her move, kissing him, essentially blowing him away, and now the ball was most decidedly in his court. So, did he answer the invitation in those soft blue eyes? Or did he do what was best for both of them, put this truck in gear and drive on home? His body was giving him one very definitive answer, his brain another. His body was winning...

"We should go home," he said.

"And then?"

The note of anticipation in her voice almost did him in.

"*I* should go home." Where he would spend the evening frustrated out of his mind.

Annie tilted up her chin. "That sounds…absolutely sensible." There was a coolness to her voice that hadn't been there before, but Trace steeled himself from reaching out and touching her, bringing the warmth back. He was going to remain sensible…even if it killed him. He couldn't allow himself to hurt this family. As near as he could figure, Annie hadn't been with anyone for years, which meant she was making an exception for him. An exception that Trace believed she would soon regret.

"Are you sure?" There was a husky note to her voice that again made him want to reach out and drag her up against him, kiss her deeply, tell her he wasn't certain at all.

Instead he said, "I'm not one to rush things." And one of them had to stay sane here. Annie had outlined very good reasons for them to remain friends only, despite the growing tension between them, and he was going to see to it that they did just that.

"I understand." Annie scooted a little farther away from him and directed her gaze forward, toward the muddy road. Her cheeks were flushed, but her expression remained cool and matter-of-fact, telling Trace that she saw the sense in what he was saying. Doing.

Once they'd reached her house, after a too-silent drive with both of them deep in thought, they unloaded the table and brought it into the shop, where Annie planned to refinish it. Then she walked him to the truck and he gave in to temptation, leaned down and gave her a quick kiss goodbye, raising his head before the heat could build. He wanted to feel those soft lips of hers beneath his one more time, because it would be the last time they kissed.

They were friends, after all. That was what Annie had asked for and that was what she was going to get. He didn't see where the other option would do anything but screw up her life when he threw his figurative saddle in the back of his truck and moved on, as he always did.

Chapter Twelve

One week after kissing Annie goodbye, Trace walked out of the Bozeman Clinic with a satisfied smile on his face. Released. For the first time ever he'd followed doctors' orders to the letter, and he had to admit, he felt ready to take on the world. He couldn't wait to get back to what he did best. Hang with his friends, as much as he hung, anyway. Get back to his life.

Earn some money.

Practice rides concerned him because, while Hennessey had some decent young bulls, most of his older stock was adequate at best. Great for training young guys, not so great when a guy needed to get ready for more challenging bulls. He was going to have to shift locales, maybe go back to Oklahoma and train there. He'd already spoken to Grady, who said that Cliff would resume chores if Trace had to leave early.

He did need to leave early because if he didn't, he'd drift back toward Annie and that wouldn't do either of them any good. He'd been foolish to think that they could act as friends, and that he could be near her—

because everything in him wanted to be near her—and not take the next logical step.

Annie had a thin line to walk between meeting her own needs and those of her kids, and to do that properly she needed to hook up with a guy who would be around. A guy she could lean on and count on being there to support her when she needed it. A guy who wasn't going to end up in the hospital or who needed to leave when that…feeling came over him. Trace wasn't that guy.

He'd felt unsettled since the day he'd first arrived in Gavin, and while his attraction to Annie and his involvement with her family had helped dampen the feeling, it was always there, just under the surface. In an odd way he wondered if that was why his shoulder had healed so well and so fast. Because he needed to get back out on the road. Back to where he was comfortable and wouldn't let anyone down.

Every now and again, though, in the days that followed that last kiss, as he kicked around the farmhouse, he found himself wishing that things were different…

They weren't. He was leaving, Annie was staying. She had responsibilities. He was responsible only for himself. That was why he'd kept his distance after delivering Annie's oak table, and he was honest enough to admit that he missed the time he'd spent with Annie and the girls. He was also honest enough to admit that he wasn't cut out for that kind of life.

Annie had made no contact with him, which told him that she understood where he was coming from, even though they hadn't discussed the matter.

Trace told himself he was good with the way things were, too.

When he reached Gavin, he stopped at the feed store for duck food. He was on his way out the door, a bag of chow under one arm, when his phone rang. A local number, so he answered.

"This is Katie."

"Uh…hi Katie. Is everything all right?"

"No." His gut tightened at her plaintive tone.

"What's wrong?" He stopped walking and stood holding the bag of duck food a few yards away from his truck.

"Can you come talk to my school? For career day."

Trace frowned down at the ground. Career day?

"Katie, I don't think that's a good idea." Not when he was doing his best to distance himself from Annie.

"It's easy," she assured him. "You stand in front of the class and the teacher and the kids ask you questions and you answer them."

"Katie…I don't talk well in front of strangers." He started walking again.

"But we need you! We were supposed to get Mr. Stewart, but he had a 'mergency and the kids want to hear about being a cowboy."

"Katie, I'm a bull rider." He hefted the grain over the side of the truck bed with one arm.

"Same thing."

"It's not the same, Katie. The kids will be disappointed not to have a real cowboy."

"But I told everyone you were coming. They 'spect you to be there."

"When?"

"After recess."

A bad thought struck him. "Are you at recess now?"

"I'm at lunch. Recess is when the clock is at two."

"Can you bring the phone to your teacher?"

"I can't."

"Why not?"

"She's not here right now."

And Katie wasn't offering any more information. Rather than pry it out of her piece by piece, Trace said, "Tell you what. I'll drop by the school. Talk to the principal."

"When?"

"In just a few minutes." He was only a couple blocks away and it seemed like the easiest solution.

"Thank you, Trace," she said in a very grown-up voice and a second later the phone went dead.

Trace hung up and dialed Annie's number. She didn't answer, so he got in the truck and drove the few blocks to the school. Once there he could talk to an adult, explain that he couldn't speak to the kids. He hated to disappoint little Katie, but he had no other choice. He couldn't exactly distance himself from the family and then show up for career day.

"I THINK YOUR daughter-in-law will enjoy the canister set, but the linens are some of my favorites." Annie took a few steps back, allowing Mrs. Helm, the manager of the bank across the street, some privacy as she considered her gift options.

"Both."

"Both?" Annie was surprised and pleased, since Mrs. Helm was a rather notorious spendthrift.

"Yes. I'll let my daughter-in-law choose between them and I'll keep whichever she doesn't choose."

Annie smiled. "Lovely idea."

"I'm remodeling my kitchen. My husband has been complaining about how dark and depressing the room is, and I've finally agreed that something needs to be done—even though it's going to be disruptive."

"Remodeling is an adventure," Annie said. Not that she'd ever done such a thing, but she'd painted, refinished and disguised, which was close. Kind of. "So many decisions to make, but it's worth it in the long run to have a cheery area to cook and eat."

"Richard promised he'd handle all of the decisions. Now he has a color scheme to work with." Mrs. Helm gestured at the matching linens and canisters.

"I do love turquoise and brown," Annie said before excusing herself to find the original canister boxes in the back room. She'd heard her phone ring a few minutes before, but had ignored it. The school or Emily would have called back on the landline, and since that hadn't happened she knew there wasn't an emergency. Not one involving her daughters, anyway.

She brought the boxes to the front counter and carefully packed the ceramic canisters back into them. She wrapped the linens in tissue, packed them in a gift box and put everything into a sturdy tote bag.

"Thank you," Mrs. Helm said after Annie handed her the receipt and her credit card. "Have a lovely day."

"You, too," Annie said, lifting her hand in a small

wave as the door closed. She started rearranging stock to cover the empty space left by the canister set and linens when the store line rang.

Annie picked up the phone on the second ring. "Annie Get Your Gun Western Boutique."

"Ms. Owen?"

Annie's heart skipped as she recognized the distinctive voice of the elementary school principal. "Yes?"

"Are you familiar with a Mr. Delaney?"

"I…am." What was going on here? Trace had all but disappeared from her life with nary a word.

"He's here at the school."

"What! Why?"

"The twins invited him to speak at career day in place of Mr. Stewart. However, we knew nothing about this substitution and you can understand our situation. We can't have guest speakers who haven't been cleared."

"I totally understand. But—" Her face was getting hot.

"I'm calling because I don't know Mr. Delaney. I've never met him or heard of him and I was certain you'd want to know that he'd been invited here by the twins, who assured me that he's a cowboy."

"Bull rider," Annie said automatically. "Could I possibly talk to Mr. Delaney? Is he still there?"

"In the front office. Wait one moment."

Annie's heart started beating harder as she waited for what seemed like an inordinately long time for Trace to say, "Hello."

"Hi. I don't know what's going on."

"Katie called and asked if I could help with career day. I tried to tell her it wasn't a good idea…" He cleared his throat as if expecting her to know what he was getting at. Well, she didn't, no more than she understood why he had disappeared from her life. "So I stopped by the school to talk to the principal and found out that things have changed a bit. You don't just walk in off the street anymore."

"I'm sorry about this." She spoke automatically as she tried to make sense of the situation.

"It's okay." His voice was deep and low and still did something to her, even though she didn't want to feel anything. He had walked away without a word. "I think the girls had good intentions. I thought it would be simple to stop by the school and discuss matters with the teacher. I didn't mean to stir up a hornet's nest."

"I'll talk with the girls."

"How about I call you back on your cell in a little bit? Mrs. Wilson wants to speak with you."

The principal came back on the line and assured Annie that she understood what had happened and that there was no harm done. Annie hung up and pressed her fingertips to her forehead.

No harm done. Right.

True to his word, Trace called her back a few minutes later.

"Where are you at?" Annie asked.

"Closing in on the city limits."

She'd hoped he was closer, close enough to stop by so that she could talk to him on neutral ground. "Once again, I apologize."

And so should he, for flat-out disappearing.

"Well, I am a cowboy." The note of humor in his voice didn't mask the underlying coolness.

"This won't happen again." Because Annie was going to have a talk with the girls, lay out a few ground rules where Mr. D'laney was concerned.

"I probably won't be around long enough for it to happen again. I got my release."

"Congratulations." Could she possibly sound more stilted and cold? Probably not. "What's your next move?"

"I'll do some practice rides at Hennessey's and then decide. My first event is in two weeks."

"Well, good luck with that." Because she wasn't going to allow herself to worry about him.

"Yes." All traces of humor were gone from his voice. "Don't...be too hard on the girls."

"As if," Annie said. "Take care, Trace."

"You, too."

Annie set down the phone before she asked him a few of the questions burning in her brain. Some things were better left unaddressed.

A few minutes later, after praying that no customers walked in, she picked the phone up and hit redial. When Trace answered, she said simply, "You know... if you're going to disappear from someone's life, you should at least say, 'Hey! Disappearing.'"

"I—"

"Because as things stand now, I'm spending way too much time wondering what happened. You said you weren't one to be rushed. You did not say you were walking away. And if I'm not mistaken, that kiss was mutual."

"Annie…"

"What?" Her voice was hard and she wished it were also cold, but it wasn't. She heard the emotion in the single word and imagined he did, too.

"I was trying to protect you," he finally said.

"Protect me?" she sputtered. "From what? Making my own decisions?" She paced through the store, trying to stem the tide of her anger, but now that she'd started venting, she didn't know if she could stop. "If you're protecting yourself, I can deal with that. But at least give me some closure. Tell me what you're doing."

"Maybe I was protecting both of us."

"Then maybe both of us should be in on the secret, Trace. You don't just take something like that into your own hands and make the decision without consulting the other party. Or at least saying, 'Goodbye. This is it.'"

There was a brief silence, then Trace said, "This is a conversation we should have in person, Annie."

"Just let me know when and where…if you dare. I have to go. A customer is at the door."

She hung up and tried to smile as an elderly lady peered in through the window before moving along to the next store.

Probably just as well, because after pouring out her feelings, she didn't know if she was ready to paste a smile on her face and pretend that all was well. Not when her nerves were buzzing and she was wondering what she'd just done. The bell on the back door rang and Danielle breezed in.

"Hey, did I miss anything?"

"The twins invited Trace to school, and campus security got him."

"What?"

Annie told the story as she tidied up displays, leaving out the part where she'd called Trace on his behavior. Danielle laughed. "Those girls are going to keep you hopping when they hit their teens."

"Thanks for the pick-me-up," Annie said with a wry smile.

She went back to her tidying, still feeling as if she had unfinished business—because she did, although there wasn't much she could do about it. As the old saying went, it took two to tango, and Trace was excusing himself from the dance. It stung, but life would go on. It always did—especially when you had kids to raise.

"MOM...IT JUST made sense," Katie said in her best adult voice as Annie backed the car out of Emily's driveway. "Mr. Stewart couldn't come and we didn't want to have to do spelling."

"You invited Trace so you didn't have to do spelling?"

"No." Katie hesitated as she always did after stretching the truth. "Well, we didn't want to do spelling, but the kids wanted to hear about being a cowboy."

"And that's the only reason you asked him?"

"He's the only cowboy we know." Kristen spoke so earnestly that all thoughts of ulterior motives evaporated from Annie's brain. There'd been no ulterior motive. No trying to ease Trace into the family.

"And he's your friend," Katie added. "He's fun to play rodeo with. He does things you don't allow us to do."

"He's our friend, too," Kristen added, making Annie's heart twist a little. "I wish we could have seen him today."

"He's almost as fun as Uncle Grady. And he never loses the bull. He should come over more often. I think he's lonely."

"No," Kristen said. "We should go over there and go riding!"

"Yeah!"

Annie sighed. "We'll hold off riding until Uncle Grady comes home, okay? And by the way, how'd you manage to call Trace?"

"We used Ella's phone at recess. Her mom lets her bring a phone to school!"

"How'd you get the number?"

"It's an easy number," Katie said. "One-two-one-two. You wrote it down by the phone, remember?"

Annie did. She'd copied it out of her cell phone onto the pad next to the landline.

"And the first part is almost like ours. Instead of six-seven-eight, it's five-seven-eight," Kristen added.

Okay… "Well…please don't call anyone without telling me first, all right? And never call anyone from school again."

"We won't…but can we invite Trace over to cook for us?"

Annie took care to monitor her tone, keep it matter-of-fact as she said, "Trace is going to leave pretty soon to ride bulls."

"He's all better?" Katie asked.

"Then he can cook for us when he comes back," Kristen said as if it were a done deal. "Maybe Lex and Uncle Grady will be back, too. We can have a big party."

The girls started discussing possibilities for homecoming celebrations, and Annie refrained from informing them that Trace wasn't likely to come back. Memories would fade and, in a matter of weeks, her life—and her girls' lives—would be the same as they'd been before her brother had invited Trace to watch his property. Busy, fulfilling, satisfying.

Oh, yes they would.

THE MORE TRACE thought about his conversation with Annie, the more irritated he became. She was the one who'd wanted to be just friends and nothing more. Well, friends didn't kiss like they kissed, so the friend thing was out the window. He'd thought it would be easier on Annie if he simply backed off for a while. Gave them both some breathing room. It wasn't like he hadn't missed her. Or that he was never going to see her again.

It wasn't like he had an easy time driving past her place every day on the way to Hennessey's. It was no easier today, after she'd lit into him, but Trace steeled himself and sailed by her mailbox. Jasper had a bull waiting for him, and he was going to ride early, before most of the crowd got there.

He'd taken months off with this injury—the longest time he'd been off during his entire career. It had to have an effect, which made him all the more determined to make up for lost time. He'd spent the last several days watching tapes, getting into his head, prepping mentally as well as physically. He'd be back in the points by the end of the year.

And he'd be able to make that event in Portland, as planned. He and Grady would be on different tours as he worked his way up through the ranks, but he'd undoubtedly run into him. That was going to feel... *Odd* was the only word he could come up with. There would be a whole new dimension to their friendship now that he'd messed up with Annie.

"You look ready," Jasper told him a half hour later.

"You have no idea." It'd felt so good to put on his gear, rosin his rope, get ready to face reality.

"Leonard here isn't our roughest bull, but he's no pansy."

"He'll do for a start." Trace eased onto the animal, situated himself, adjusted his rope, his grip. An aura of sheer strength rose up out of the animal, surrounding him, and Trace did his best to tap into it, use it to his advantage.

He nodded and the gate swung open. Leonard took one mighty leap out of the chute then short hopped and started to spin. Trace pushed down through his feet, countered the spin and refused to think about his shoulder. He'd told Jasper he was going for ten seconds instead of eight, even though it was his first ride. Ten because if he could do ten, then he knew for certain he could do eight.

Bill blew his whistle and Trace disembarked easily. Leonard didn't give Trace a second look once he was on the ground. The big bull trotted over to the gate and waited for it to open. Trace picked up his rope and grinned at Jasper, who gave an approving nod. No, Leonard wasn't the toughest bull around, but he wasn't the easiest, either. It was a good start.

Trace rode again that practice, hitting the dirt before ten seconds had elapsed, and jarring his shoulder, but it didn't send that bone-numbing pain shooting through him that he'd experienced every single ride before the surgery. This was just normal pain. He decided to leave well enough alone and call it a day.

"You won't be around for much longer, will you?" Jasper asked as Trace left the practice pen.

"Nope. I'm going to Portland and from there I'm heading back to Oklahoma. My friend there just bought a smaller place, but he still has a practice pen."

"It's been good having you."

"I'm not gone yet."

Jasper gave a short shake of his head as if he didn't quite believe him. Trace dusted off and headed to his truck. Cody drove in as he was pulling out and Trace lifted his hand to wave. They were almost ten years apart in age, but one thing they had in common, other than bull riding, was that neither of them had a chance with Annie. Cody had no chance because Annie wasn't interested in him, and Trace had no chance because he wasn't going to seek one. He knew what was best for both of them.

The thought stopped him cold.

That was exactly what Annie had been angry about. His deciding what was best for both of them. He'd understood why she felt that way when they'd spoken on the phone, yet he'd still stubbornly believed that he'd done the right thing. He'd done it the wrong way, but the outcome was the same—Annie was protected—and he'd been willing to live with that.

Until now.

How insulted would he be if someone assumed that he needed protection without his permission or knowledge? Because they thought they knew best.

Pretty damned insulted. Just as Annie had been.

ANNIE STOPPED UNPACKING groceries and went to the window when she heard the crunching sound of tires on gravel. Trace.

Why?

Because she needed more frustration ammunition?

Well, she was at capacity, thank you very much. She drew herself up and stepped out onto the porch as Trace got out of his truck. Before she could speak, though, he raised his chin to meet her gaze and the expression on his face stalled out whatever it was she'd been about to say.

"We need to talk," he said simply. "And I believe you dared me to come by."

Annie swallowed the sudden dryness in her throat. She had dared him, and she couldn't back out now.

"Are the girls here?" he asked, following her back into the house. Annie shook her head as he shut the door. "Good."

As per usual, a moment of awkward silence hung between them that neither attempted to break. As far as Annie was concerned, he'd accepted the dare, so she'd let him start, because she wasn't certain where to begin—or even where she'd left off.

"I was trying to make things easier by disappearing."

The note of quiet regret in his voice almost did her in. "I know you were, Trace. That's the hell of it."

"Like I said before, friends don't kiss like that."

"Well, maybe I changed my mind about being friends."

"And maybe I thought you'd come to regret that."

Annie tilted her chin up. "Maybe we should have talked about it. Maybe I should have told you with words that I was changing my mind. Although, I thought I'd made it pretty obvious."

"I was—still am—afraid of hurting you, Annie."

"Why? Because you don't think I can handle it?"

"No. Because I care for you."

Her heart stuttered. Before she could answer, he went on, "I am leaving. It's a given. I had my first ride today. It was good. In two weeks I'll be in Portland. Next month I'll be in Austin. I'll be back in Oklahoma during my off time where I can train on decent bulls."

Annie lifted her eyebrows in a cool expression. "Maybe I'm good with that."

"Maybe?"

"As in, I don't know, Trace. I've never experienced

anything like this. I've never had a whirlwind affair. I've never had a husband. I've never had a lot of things. I think I want one thing, then come to find out I want another."

He studied her with an ever-deepening frown.

"Translation?" he finally asked softly.

Annie lifted her hands in surrender. She had no idea how to articulate all the contradictions that kept shooting through her brain.

Trace moved a few steps closer, close enough that she wondered if she could feel the warmth from his body or if she was just imagining it. "When you kissed me…" she said softly, letting her gaze drop down to his perfect lips, remembering that kiss and somehow losing track of what she was trying to say in the process.

"The time wasn't right," he finally murmured when it became clear that she couldn't find words.

"The location was a problem, if I recall."

"And me. I was a problem."

"Somewhat," she agreed.

"Here's the thing… Annie, you are the most grounded person I know. I didn't want things to get out of hand. I didn't want you to regret anything. On that day I thought I was being noble, but what I was really doing was making the decision for both of us."

"Without asking what I wanted."

"Without asking what you wanted." He reached out to trace his fingers down her cheek, setting all of her nerves on fire. "What do you want, Annie?"

"I honestly thought I wanted just friendship. Before. It seemed…sensible. Safe. Sane."

"And now?"

She moistened her lips before saying, "I want to experience some things that are not tied to being a mom and a sister and a good friend." The total truth. She wanted to spread her wings, like other women. Expand her world.

"You said that thing about not liking people who say things they don't mean and make promises they don't keep."

"That's true. I can't handle that."

"I've always been truthful to you, Annie. I always will be. Even if it's a truth you don't want to hear."

"I'll do the same." She sucked in a breath as his fingers moved slowly along her jawline. "So…here goes. I want you."

Something glinted in his eyes as she spoke. "That's laying it out there."

"I won't get anywhere hinting."

"Actually, that's an area where I do take a hint."

"You didn't last time," she pointed out. Her heart was starting to beat harder. Faster.

"Again, I was being noble." He lifted the corner of his mouth. "Won't do that again." His expression softened as he brought his hands up to frame her face, lowering his forehead to touch hers. "Where are the girls?"

"Birthday party."

"Are you telling me that for once in my life I might be in the right place at the right time?"

Annie leaned in to brush her mouth against his. He smiled beneath her touch. "Maybe this once."

"How long do we have?"

Annie met his eyes, hoping he could see just how serious she was when she said, "Long enough for you to show me all the stuff I've been missing for all these years."

"Enough said." He took her lips in a deep, deep kiss, slowly backing her up. Annie felt the edge of the counter against her back, but more than that, she felt the pressure of his mouth, the amazing sensations of his tongue, the strength of his hands as they held her at her waist. His thumbs brushed up over her rib cage, close to her breasts, but not close enough.

Annie sighed against his mouth then wrapped her arms around his neck and pulled him even closer.

He slowly lifted his head, looking down at her through hooded eyes. "Just so you know, we can stop whenever you want… Like I said, I'm not one to rush things."

"Thank you, but I don't think I'll need to stop."

He simply smiled and took her lips again, and even though the sensations were making her crazy, urging her to take and be taken, Annie was supremely aware of the fact that she was rusty in this area, too. Beyond rusty. She hadn't had all that much experience before Wes left, and absolutely zero experience after.

But as Trace skimmed his hands up over her breasts, nuzzled her neck, nipped her earlobe, thoughts of what she hadn't done were soon replaced with thoughts of what she was going to do. Her breath caught as he lifted her up onto the counter, putting them eye to eye. She settled her hands on his broad shoulders, felt the tension and strength playing beneath her palms, and the thought of feeling him naked against her made her insides start to spiral.

"I...uh—" she closed her eyes as he pressed a warm kiss against her jawline "—have a bedroom, you know."

Trace lifted her off the counter and she automatically wrapped her legs around his waist to keep her balance. "Right or left at the doorway?" he asked.

"Right."

Somehow Annie got the word out before his mouth closed over hers and he started walking.

Chapter Thirteen

Annie's red terry-cloth robe didn't fit Trace all that well, but it covered him while they sat on the sofa and pretended to watch television. Trace was in no hurry to leave and Annie was in no hurry to see him go. The robe dropped away from one muscular leg as he propped his foot onto the ottoman and flipped through the television channels. Annie tried to focus on the viewing options as they flew by—really, she did—but instead found her gaze straying to his partially exposed leg.

She'd thought he had no scars, but it turned out he had no visible scars. His thigh was a mess, even though he assured her that no arteries had been compromised when he'd been hooked by a young bull as a sixteen-year-old. There was a very neat surgical scar on his shoulder and another above one knee, but other than that, he was actually in good shape.

Excellent shape.

Would-love-to-get-her-hands-back-on-him shape.

Trace's phone buzzed and he reached for it then got to his feet and left the room as he spoke bull-riding business. A few minutes later he came back wearing his jeans and tucking in his T-shirt, his feet still bare.

Annie shook her head. "I kind of liked the other look."

"You've had all the looking you're going to get for today," he said gruffly, his eyes glinting with amusement. Annie answered him by tossing a pillow at his midsection.

"Easy now," he said, catching the pillow and tossing it away before sitting back beside her. "I don't want to risk injury."

Annie snorted and Trace smiled that devastating smile that made her wish she wasn't picking up the twins in an hour as he sat back on the sofa and hauled her onto his lap. Annie pushed her hands into his hair and met his lips.

She still had half an hour before she had to leave, and life had taught her long ago that it was best to take advantage of opportunity while it was there.

Half an hour later Annie was dressed and Trace was dressed once again. She felt alive and inspired and... good. Very, very good. Sex was indeed like riding a bicycle, except that it felt a whole lot better, before, during and after.

"You know," Trace said after opening the door to his truck, "I could bring dinner over tomorrow. I have a free morning and you don't."

"That would be great."

"What do you think...something with turnips and mustard?"

Annie laughed. "I don't think the girls would be very happy with Mr. D'laney."

"What would you like?" he said, ambling closer for a kiss.

"I would like something simple and easy to make and—" she took hold of the front of his shirt "—maybe a little more time alone."

His expression brightened briefly, then he smiled ruefully. "That's not going to happen tomorrow, is it?"

She gave her head a slow shake. "Afraid not. All you'll get is scintillating company and a possible game of rodeo."

He gave her one last kiss before stepping away. "I'll take it."

"And you know what?" Annie said. "I'll cook. I have a frozen homemade casserole. That way you can concentrate on your tapes and all that other stuff you do to prepare to get the snot beat out of you."

"Spoken like a bull rider's sister."

AFTER THE RODEO game and then dinner the next night, the girls happily ensconced themselves in front of the television while Trace did the dishes. Annie dried and after a quick glance to make certain the coast was clear, Trace put an arm around her then let his hand drift down to the curve of her hip.

Annie leaned into him and Trace took her lips in a quick kiss before putting both hands back into the water. He heard Annie inhale deeply then exhale as she took a dish from him, rinsed it and dried it.

"You shouldn't be helping. You cooked."

"Defrosted and baked," she corrected. "And I like doing this."

As did he. It was new territory, having to check for kids prior to making a move on an attractive woman, but he didn't mind.

"You should come back the day after tomorrow," Annie said.

"Yeah?"

"The girls have a slumber party in town."

"I'll be here," Trace promised with a waggle of his dark eyebrows.

"I thought you might. Only—" she gave him a sideways look "—this time you're cooking. I'd like macaroni and cheese, please. With mustard."

He tipped her chin up with one soapy finger and lightly kissed her lips. "Done."

TRACE SPENT THE next two evenings at Annie's house. He wanted more time alone with her, but it wasn't to be, so he took what he could get—and he enjoyed it. In less than a week, he'd be gone. He was just glad that he and Annie were on the same page. It was obvious to him that she enjoyed being with him as much as he loved being with her. And the thing that made him most relieved was that they'd part on good terms. In a contrary way, he looked forward to going, even though he'd miss Annie like crazy, because the longer he stayed, the more chances he had to screw up. Hurt this family.

But the days passed and no emotional disasters occurred. He thought he was home free—was actually congratulating himself—and then Kristen announced at dinner that she'd gotten an extra chair at the school play for him. She radiated excitement as she announced her coup. Trace shot a look at Annie, who instantly understood his dilemma.

"I'm not going to be here," he said gently.

"Not going to be here?" the twins said in unison. "But it's our play!"

"I'll be traveling to Portland."

Kristen's lip started to shake, and Trace felt a moment of panic.

"Ladies, I told you that Trace had events coming up and that he couldn't come to your play."

"But that was when you were mad at him."

Annie stared at her girls with a stunned expression then quickly recovered. "Nothing has changed."

"You're friends again, and we thought for sure that Trace was coming."

"I can't come, sweetie. I want to."

Katie's mouth clamped shut and she lowered her eyes. "Humph."

Trace's stomach knotted and he had to remind himself that it was just a play. Important to the girls, but a play about butterflies and squirrels.

"Ladies…" Annie said in a warning tone.

The girls both picked up their forks and started to eat, their movements slow and unenthusiastic. Annie sighed and met Trace's eyes.

He felt terrible.

"They'll get over it," she said later as he was packing up leftovers for her.

"I have to go to my event."

She looked at him in surprise. "The girls need to understand that not everything works out the way they want it to." Her mouth tightened a little and he had a feeling she was going to say more, but his phone rang. He answered it with a clipped hello, then his voice changed. "Sure. Yeah. We can discuss it tomorrow. No, I planned to be there. I won't ride, but I'll be there."

Annie crossed the floor to him as he dropped his phone into his pocket. She didn't say a word as she rose up on her toes and kissed him deeply. Trace's breath caught as his hands closed over her shoulders.

Damn but this woman could do things to him.

SHE'D ALMOST DONE IT. She'd almost asked Trace why he felt the need to move on, to keep from putting down roots, even when the circumstances might be conducive to rooting.

She'd almost asked what it was he was running from.

But it wasn't the time, so she'd walked him to the door after kissing him and let him go on his way. And then she'd watched his taillights until they disappeared into the distance. What had she gotten herself into?

Nothing that she regretted, she told herself firmly. Better to have loved and lost and all that. She wouldn't give up one day she'd spent with Trace…and they did so well together, the four of them. Was it possible or realistic to wonder if Trace might not realize what he was missing after he left?

Or was he going to settle back into his old life and simply remember her and her girls fondly?

Yes, she could hope. She could question. The one thing she couldn't do was to try to change his course of action. She'd learned long ago that when a person needed to do something, you had to stand back and let them. Grady and bull riding. Her father and trucking. Wes and his rodeo. People did what they had to do. What they were wired to do.

The girls forgave Trace for missing the play not that long after he'd driven away.

"He can see our play next year," Kristen decreed. "We'll have our teachers put it on a day when he doesn't have a 'vent." Because in her mind, Trace had become like Grady—he might leave to ride bulls, but he would come back.

"E-vent," Annie corrected. "And he has another home in Oklahoma, so after he leaves, he might not be back for a long time." Not totally true about the home in Oklahoma, but close enough. Trace had a home wherever he laid his head down, according to him.

Kristen gave her mother a solemn look. "He'll be back."

Annie nodded and turned toward the fridge to put away the leftovers. Maybe he would…but only after he figured a few things out.

Tourist season was ramping up and Annie Get Your Gun experienced a nice uptick in sales. The quilt room was so successful that Danielle was now taking consignment items from other local quilters.

Annie was rearranging stock to cover the empty spot left by a very satisfying sale when the bell rang and Mrs. Hennessey came in with Mrs. Wilson, the school principal. Danielle greeted them and guided them to the area where they'd stocked gifts suitable for graduation.

It didn't take the ladies long to choose Western-themed cards and jewelry for their graduates, and Annie rang up the sale while Danielle went to the back to wrap.

"Lovely stock as usual," Mrs. Wilson said.

Annie smiled and started to respond when Mrs. Hennessey said, "Too bad about your young man. Jasper tried to keep him here, you know, but he turned him down."

Annie blinked at her. "My...young man?"

Mrs. Hennessey lifted finely groomed gray eyebrows. "Don Maguire said...some things."

She smiled meaningfully and Annie looked heavenward. The bull rider who'd witnessed the windows they'd steamed up after the trailer wreck. She cleared her throat. "Well, I appreciate the effort."

What else could she do, other than melt into the floor? Floor melting was actually an inviting option, given the fact that Principal Wilson was listening to the conversation with keen interest.

"It wasn't a mercy job he offered, either. Jasper says your young man is a natural teacher and good with the stock."

"Yes," Annie muttered as Danielle came out from the back with two beautifully wrapped boxes. "He's quite talented, but you know how it is with bull riders. The road calls."

So loudly apparently that Trace had turned down the opportunity to stay even seasonally. That hurt. A lot.

Annie pressed her lips together as the women strolled out.

"So…you and Trace?" Danielle asked as she tidied up the stack of paper bags near the register.

Annie turned weary eyes to her friend. "Temporary thing. That's all. He's leaving in a matter of days and won't be back."

"You're good with that."

Annie considered then gave an abrupt nod. "I am."

As IT TURNED OUT, Trace didn't have to ask Cliff, the neighbor, to feed Lex's animals for more than a couple of days. Grady called to tell Trace that he and Lex were coming home for a couple of weeks while he recovered from a strained elbow. So that was one issue solved.

The thing with Annie… He didn't know about that, but all seemed well so far. He hadn't been able to stop by the previous evening, but he'd called to tell her he wouldn't be there. She'd been fine with it, reinforcing what she'd said about just needing to know—which was why he was going to be up-front about Hennessey's job offer. An offer that had surprised the heck out of him.

An offer that wouldn't work for a number of reasons—Hennessey's stock wasn't gnarly enough and Trace wasn't ready to settle into a job. Not yet. Not here.

That evening, after they'd finished dinner and had cleaned the kitchen, and while the twins were in the living room watching a princess-somebody show, Annie backed Trace up against the kitchen counter. She took his face in her hands, pulled his lips down to hers for a kiss, as she so often did. Only this kiss felt different. Serious.

When she leaned back, she said, "I want to come clean and tell you that I know about Hennessey's job offer. His wife told me."

Trace's mouth tightened. "I was going to tell you tonight."

"So I figured." She spoke with a sincerity that told him she believed him. "It didn't seem right to have you working out how to tell me something I already know."

"I couldn't take the job, Annie. It doesn't mesh with my plans."

"What are your plans?"

"Portland. Austin. St. Louis."

"And then?"

"I'll find a place to land for a month or two then hit the road again. Like I always do. Stoddard, the Oklahoma guy—"

"I know who he is," Annie said. "Grady once worked for him, too."

"He's in the process of buying another place. I'll probably end up bunking with him again because his bulls are better than Hennessey's are. He plans to have a state-of-the-art practice facility."

She glanced down, pressing her lips together, looking as if she were fighting emotion.

"Annie," he said, feeling a swell of irritation mixed with regret. "This was the plan from the beginning."

She raised her eyes then to meet his gaze. Her expression was oddly calm.

"Yes."

She didn't say anything else, which made Trace want to fill the void. But with what would he fill it? Reiterations of the fact that he'd always said he was leaving? She wasn't arguing that.

"You have to admit that my staying would be complicated. I mean…I love the time we've had, but we have to be realistic."

"Yes."

Trace pressed his lips together, wishing she would argue with him. Annie took a step back, smoothing her hands down the front of his shirt before dropping them to her sides.

"Why do you have this thing about moving on, Trace?"

"I was raised on the move. Even in Reno, we moved all the time, chasing cheap rent. It's all I know."

"And you can't learn anything else?"

He leaned back, regarding her from half-closed eyes. "I'm not going to try and fail, using you and Katie and Kristen as test subjects. You even said you didn't want that to happen." While they'd worked out their friendship agreement at her kitchen table, weeks ago. She might have changed what she wanted for herself, but he sincerely doubted that she'd changed what she wanted for her girls.

She drew in a breath and he knew she was going to say, "But what if you don't fail," before the words came out of her mouth. When they did, he shook his head.

"I can't take the chance with you guys. I don't think I can be what you need me to be." He swallowed hard. "I *know* I can't be what you need me to be."

A look of extreme sadness crossed her face, then slowly she nodded. "I guess there's not much else to say, is there?"

TRACE LEFT THE day before Grady and Lex came home, even though it was still a few days before his Portland comeback rodeo.

Annie told herself that it was best that he left when he did, before she lost the battle with herself and tried to argue him into staying. The girls were stunned, however, to discover that Trace had left, just as he'd said he would. Apparently they'd clung to the belief that his event would get canceled or that he would come to his senses and realize that a butterfly play was far more important than an event in which he could win thousands of dollars.

"He couldn't miss his event," Lex said in a no-nonsense way as she helped the twins get ready backstage. "He has to start making his living again. He told you he had to leave, right?"

"Right," Katie agreed.

Annie's mouth tightened.

True to his word, Trace hadn't made a single promise he hadn't kept. She couldn't say the same, since she'd promised herself she'd be satisfied with whatever she got out of the relationship. She hadn't expected to fall in love with the guy. She hadn't expected to want more than he was capable of giving. He'd been honest, so this was all on her. She'd allowed herself to believe that he would come to understand how great it was to be part of a family—a secret hope she hadn't fully acknowledged until he was gone.

"You look amazing," Lex said as she knelt down in front of Kristen to retie her sash and help her adjust her glittery scarf wings. Oddly, it was fearless Kristen who was suffering from stage fright rather than Katie, who was humming under her breath as Annie pinned her antennae headband into place.

"What if I forget my lines?" Kristen asked.

Oh, yeah, this had all the earmarks of a disaster.

"Then you'll be in good company," Lex said before Annie could answer. Kristen tilted her head and Lex continued, "Every great actor has forgotten lines."

"Even Princess Bettina?" Katie asked.

Lex nodded solemnly, even though Princess Bettina was digitally animated.

"If you forget your lines," Annie said, "Mrs. Lawrence will whisper the first few words to you from behind the curtain. Remember?"

"Or you could just make something up," Lex said. "It's called improvising. Lots of actors do it."

Annie truly hoped it didn't come to that.

"Parents," Mrs. Lawrence said as she came into the room. "It's time for you to take your seats out front. Actors, positions, please."

Lex and Annie took turns hugging the girls, then left the stage area to take the seats that Grady had saved them front and center. Grady shifted in his chair and

Annie got the distinct feeling that he was as nervous as Kristen.

"They'll do fine," he said as she sat beside him.

Annie hoped so. As it was, she had to wait for almost five minutes before the twins came on stage as the first vanguard of the butterfly patrol. Kristen fluttered her scarf wings, but Katie, who'd been so nonchalant about the performance, looked out over the audience and froze. Her eyes grew large and Annie had the distinct feeling that her daughter was about to clamber down the stairs at the edge of the stage.

"She's going to bolt," she said to Grady.

Before she took flight, the boy in the rabbit suit nudged Katie and repeated his line. She turned toward him as if surprised to see him. He said his line a third time. Katie blinked a couple of times then said, "I'm so glad to be in the forest today," before turning to look back out over the audience.

"Mrs. Lawrence," the boy whispered loudly, shooting a glance toward the heavy backstage curtain, "she said the wrong line."

A collective chuckle went up from the audience and then Kristen said to him, "If you forget your line, you're *supposed* to make something up."

Lex pressed her lips together, but her shoulders were shaking as she shot Annie an apologetic look, then Grady leaned close to whisper, "Perfect kid plays are boring. This is entertainment."

Annie had to agree. A few ad-libs were preferable to stilted dialogue, although it, too, had its charm when delivered by seven-year-olds.

There was a murmur behind the curtain and Katie squared her shoulders and said, "I hope the other butterflies find us soon, before we have to fly to our new home for the summer."

On cue several children in colorful scarves whirled onto the stage, and the twins joined their band of butterfly brothers and sisters, dancing and swirling before leaving the stage. Annie's shoulders sagged in relief. Now she could relax until the end of the performance when the group song ended the play.

After the song, the children joined hands and bowed deeply, then raced off stage. Not long after that, they came spilling out of the stage side door and joined their proud parents.

"I was so proud of how you handled it when you forgot your line," Annie said as she hugged Katie.

"I thought I saw Trace, but it wasn't him."

Annie's heart lurched. "When did you think you saw Trace?"

"When I forgot my line. But it was Vanessa's dad. His hat is like Trace's hat."

Annie let out a small sigh. They all missed Trace. He'd left a hole in their lives, but things would get better.

They couldn't get much worse.

Chapter Fourteen

Trace stretched as he waited for his bull to settle in the chute. He'd been lucky enough to draw Bumblebee, a tough little bull who could be counted on to get a guy into the money. He climbed onboard and fixed his grip then nodded at the gatekeeper. The gate opened and Bumblebee didn't move. The gate closed again.

"Keep going?"

Trace nodded. He didn't know what the deal was, but he'd never seen Bumblebee balk before. Once again the gate opened and this time Bumblebee reared out of the chute, but he wasn't feeling it tonight. He began a series of lackluster short jumps followed by one high buck then a couple more short jumps. The whistle blew and Trace disembarked, jarring his shoulder on the landing. Bumblebee stopped bucking and trotted toward the gate, leaving Trace staring after him in disgust. It wasn't bad enough to garner a reride, but it was bad enough to keep him out of the standings.

Thanks, Bumblebee.

He kept his head down as he strode toward the gate and left the arena. Not in the points, not in the money.

Two events in a row. This was not the comeback he'd hoped for.

"Maybe you'll draw better next week." He turned to see Grady walking a few steps behind him.

"Here's hoping," he agreed. Trace had no idea how much Grady knew about what had happened between him and Annie, but he got the idea his friend was none too pleased with him.

"So you're going to St. Louis."

"Where else would I be going?"

"I know where you probably shouldn't go."

"Where's that?" Trace asked, pushing his hat back as he spoke.

"You probably shouldn't go back to Gavin." Trace started to speak, but Grady cut him off. "I don't know what happened with you and my sister, but she's not happy. And my nieces aren't happy. When I offered you my place, I hadn't expected you to screw with my family."

"That's the last thing I wanted to do."

"Good. Because you're not getting a second chance at it." Trace felt something twist hard inside his gut at Grady's adamant tone. "You need to stay away from her."

"And you need to let Annie fight her own battles." They both turned to see Lex standing behind them, one hand propped on her hip.

"Lex…"

She appeared unimpressed with the warning in her fiancé's voice. Their gazes clashed for a moment, and then Grady turned back to Trace. "My fiancée and

I disagree on this matter, but I still want you to stay away from her."

What if I don't?

Trace bit back the words and even though Lex had seemingly supported him, when he met her gaze, it was hard and unyielding and again his gut twisted. He'd done the right thing. Yes, the time with Annie and her girls had been special, but it'd been a moment out of time. The equivalent of a summer romance. It killed him, though, to think that he'd caused them pain. That hadn't been on the agenda. That had been the freaking reason he'd left.

Someone hailed Grady, and even though their business wasn't fully dealt with, Trace took the opportunity to head to the locker room. If Grady wanted to discuss the matter further, he knew where to find him.

ANNIE PACED THROUGH the store, shifting the jewelry, redraping towels over the edge of the open steamer trunk, hanging a child's cowboy hat with a beaded hatband on a wall hook then taking it back off again. As she went for the broom for the third time that day, Danielle said, "Stop."

Annie turned with the broom in her hand as Danielle came out from behind the counter. Gently Danielle took the broom from her and set it back in the corner. "We need tea."

"I'm fine—"

"Tea," Danielle said firmly. She filled the electric kettle. "Sit." She waved at the chairs and Annie wondered if it was wrong to hope that a customer would come in right now to save her.

Why do you need saving?

A question she didn't want to answer any more than she wanted to sit and drink herbal tea instead of pacing madly through the store tidying and rearranging. And that meant that she needed to do exactly what she'd been trying to teach the twins to do…face up to the fact that if you feel like hiding something—a broken glass, a rip in your best dress—there's a good chance that you need to confront whatever it is dead-on, deal with the consequences and keep going rather than let it eat at you.

Annie sat in her regular chair at the antique table where they held their business meetings every Wednesday morning. Danielle placed a delicate tea cup in front of her and a few minutes later poured hot water into the teapot. They sat in silence as the mint tea steeped, then Danielle served them both.

"I apologize for not being myself."

Danielle's lips curved slightly, but she didn't say anything before she sipped her tea.

"I'll be fine in a day or two." Or maybe a week or two. *Year* or two. How had she become so attached to a man who'd been so honest about leaving?

"I miss Trace." There. She'd come right out and said it. He'd been gone for over a month, but she'd just heard from Grady that he was paired up with Brick again at an exhibition performance and she was worried.

"Are you going to do something about it?"

"Missing him? What can I do? I can't force him to settle down."

"No. You can't." Danielle took another sip. "Force never works."

"People need to do what they need to do."

"I found that out with Grady. He needed to ride bulls more than he needed me."

"I guess you did." Her brother's former engagement to Danielle used to be a subject she avoided, until she finally realized that she felt more sensitive about it than Danielle did.

"However..." She drew the word out then set down her teacup. "That's not to say that people always know what they need to do."

"Meaning?"

Danielle gave a small shrug. "Sometimes people are afraid of following a certain path for reasons that have nothing to do with the path itself."

"I can't change those reasons."

"But you can challenge them."

Annie slowly shook her head. She'd tried challenging reasons more than once in her life and had come up a sorry loser every time. If she'd had her way, her brother wouldn't have gotten back on a bull after the first time he ended up in the hospital. But trying to change Grady's mind about bull riding had been like trying to change the course of a tornado. She'd tried to change Wes's mind when he told her that he wasn't ready for fatherhood. A lot of good that had done her. He'd skipped out during the night, never to be heard from again, except for the quarterly child support checks that came into the bank like clockwork. He truly didn't want to risk having contact with his children.

And then there'd been her father. *Please, Dad. Spend less time on the road.* He hadn't. It had broken her mother's heart.

"Some things you have to accept," she said in a low voice. "When someone makes a decision about their life, then you have to take it as it is and hope for the best."

"What if it's the wrong decision?"

"Who am I to decide that?"

Danielle picked up her cup. "Someone with a vested interest." Annie drew in a breath before Danielle continued, "I think he loves you. I think he's pretty scared of that fact."

"I do, too." Annie set down her tea, barely touched, as the bell over the door rang. "I appreciate the tea and concern, but I am all right. I just need to grieve." She gave a small smile. "Part of the healing process."

She'd made it sound so easy and so matter-of-fact when it was anything but. She'd been in love before. She'd been in love with Wes. Her world had shattered when he'd left and she'd thought it would never be whole again. But it was, and if anything, she was stronger and happier for knowing that she could survive heartbreak and come out whole. She'd done it once, and she could do it again.

She didn't have a choice.

The afternoon passed slowly. Even though she desperately wanted to move, to do something, Annie refrained from rearranging and pacing, for fear of having more tea pressed upon her. Trace was going to ride Brick, she was going to continue her life and, eventually, all would be well.

Because she was going to make it well. Somehow.

The girls were bubbling over with excitement when Annie picked them up. Emily had gotten a new puppy and they'd had the time of their lives playing with him. Discussing the possibility of getting a puppy themselves kept Annie busy on the drive home and by the time she started dinner, she was able to tell herself that this was what was important—being a good mom, making a nice home for her daughters. They had accepted the fact that Trace was gone much better than she had, and she'd quickly realized that she didn't need to project her heartbreak onto them.

Heartbreak.

She hated how often that word popped into her head. She was not heartbroken. She was hurting and only because she'd allowed herself to fall in love.

And because Trace Delaney was too scarred to change his chosen course in life.

Scarred or scared?

Did it matter? The result was the same.

And what about you? a small voice asked. *Aren't you scarred and scared, too?*

Maybe.

Yes.

She'd tried to force Wes to settle down and it hadn't worked. That had been a huge lesson. He'd stayed as long as he could, went through the motions, but when she was three months pregnant he had bolted.

Because as gorgeous and fun as he had been, he hadn't had a lot of integrity or loyalty. Life was all about him.

You do choose them well.

"TELL ME HOW you feel facing the bull that took you out at the end of the last season."

The television lady pushed the microphone closer to his face and Trace said, "I feel like I have a chance for vindication."

"And the shoulder. How's it feeling after the surgery?"

"Better than before. I'd put it off for too long. Maybe I owe old Brick a debt of gratitude. If it hadn't been for him I might have put it off even longer."

"Great attitude, Trace. Good luck with the ride."

"Thank you."

Honestly, he was going to need it. Brick was undefeated this season. No one had ridden him for longer than six seconds. Trace had every intention of getting his eight.

He just had to focus. Go through the ride mentally. Prepare for all eventualities.

Get Annie out of his head.

That was the challenge. She was with him constantly, and she was with him now. Distracting him in a way he didn't need to be distracted. Nothing like this had ever happened to him before, but he was certain that he'd move past this with time.

"Delaney! You're up!"

The shout snapped him back to the present. He

started toward the chute, giving his shoulder one more roll for reassurance. Fine. He felt fine. Brick banged around in the chute, kicking with one hind foot. Trace leaned over the rail, adjusted his rope. Brick rolled his eye at him, as if to say, "You're mine."

"Right back at you," Trace muttered before he climbed on board.

Brick shifted irritably as Trace settled, twitching the skin on his back as if Trace were an annoying fly. He shifted his hips, wrapped the rope, pounded his glove. Deep breath, eyes closed. Weight in his feet. Center of the bull.

He gave a quick nod and the gate opened.

The next thing he knew he was at the end of his arm—Brick had blasted out of the chute that fast, and from there, Trace was playing catch up. Before he could get his weight back where he wanted it, in his feet, Brick spun away from his hand and then tossed him forward, swinging him around and smashing him into the ground.

Trace automatically started scrambling, trying to get out from under the bull, catching flashes of hooves and horns as the bullfighters ran toward him. For a brief moment he thought he was home free, just before he caught the hoof to the side of his head and went down...

THE GOOD NEWS was that he'd be healed in time for the second half of the tour, which started in late August, just as he'd planned from the beginning. He'd also get another shot at Brick in December at Man vs. Bull.

The bad news was that he was going to be out for several weeks. Again.

The worst news was that he didn't care.

What had happened to him?

Easy answer. Annie. The girls. A glimpse of a life he'd long ago told himself he couldn't have. He'd had security snatched away from him so many times that he'd been afraid to believe he could have it.

Tough. Tenacious. That was how the announcer had described him after the ride.

Bull.

He'd gotten scared of having what he wanted yanked away from him again and had hit the road rather than fight for it. He'd behaved like a freaking coward and that didn't sit well with him. The biggest problem was that until he worked things out with Annie—settled them one way or the other, faced his fear of loss...well, his career was going to suffer.

He was going to suffer.

And right now, as the meds kicked in, he was going to pass out. When he came out of it, he'd call Stoddard, make sure he had a bunk. Then when he was healed, he'd head to Gavin. Risk Grady's protective-brother wrath. He was done running. Well and truly done.

His eyes slowly closed as his limbs grew heavy.

He was...drifting.

ANNIE HAD NEVER spent more than a night away from her girls, but right now she was planning to spend at least two nights away from home. More if she had to. She and Trace were going to have words. And if he was weak because of the medication and pain, good. She was not above taking advantage.

Lex had texted shortly after Annie arrived in Salt Lake City, assuring her that the girls were fine and quite busy cleaning all of Lex's tack. And Lex owned a lot of tack. With her mind eased on that score, Annie focused on her mission.

She parked in the hospital lot and went into the cafeteria to get a cup of coffee before embarking on her mission. It'd been a long drive from Gavin and she needed a minute to regroup. This, she figured, might be her last chance to talk sense into a stubborn man who was scared to death of hurting her. Failing her.

As if.

It had taken time, going over their previous conversations, having several heart-to-hearts with stern and protective Grady before she'd fully accepted that it was probably fear that motivated her man. Fear of losing. Fear of failing those he loved. He hadn't been able to keep his mom alive. He hadn't been welcome at his dad's ranch. He'd moved around, making few friends until he'd started riding bulls. Even the couple who'd mentored him had passed away.

The guy had nothing permanent in life.

Well, he was going to have something permanent now.

After her coffee, which had to be the reason her heart was beating harder than usual, she went to the desk and asked for Trace's room number then took an elevator to the second floor. By the time she approached the room, her heart was hammering to the point that she could no longer blame caffeine. She was scared. Really scared.

When Grady had told her that Trace had been hurt again, she'd almost thrown up. And that had convinced her once and for all that she was not going to let him ruin both of their lives. Not without one heck of a struggle. She pushed the door open, sucking in a breath as she saw Trace lying in the bed closest to the door. The other bed was empty.

Good. No witnesses.

She lifted her chin and moved into the room.

Let the battle begin.

TRACE HEARD THE nurse come in and slowly opened his eyes…only to discover that he was hallucinating. It wasn't a nurse who stood next to his bed. It was Annie. His mouth was dry, but he managed to say, "Are you here to prop me up?"

"I'm here to take you home."

If he'd had a heart monitor on, it would have redlined.

"I don't have a home."

"Yeah. You do."

"I'm not going to be taken in like some charity case."

"I think you know better than that."

Damn, but she looked adamant. Trace closed his eyes and wished the pain meds hadn't worn off. At least then he'd be loopy and could blame these feelings on the drugs. But his mind was clear and he had no doubt about Annie's meaning.

She leaned down and took his chin in her hand, holding it as she stared into his eyes. His breath caught at the fierceness in her expression. "I've come for what's mine. Whatever fears you have about not having what it takes to be a decent partner, we'll confront. Together. But the one thing I know is that you are a good man. Wes left because he was worried about himself. You left because you were worried about me. About failing me and the girls."

Trace swallowed. True. At least the part about him being afraid of failure.

"All right," he said slowly. "I left because I was scared. Scared of screwing up. Scared of hurting you and the girls. Scared of not being enough."

"And that's where you got yourself into trouble," Annie said darkly. "When you have doubts, you voice them."

"I did."

"And then I made my mistake. I let you go." Her expression shifted, softened. "Come home with me, Trace. We need you."

He looked at the wall over Annie's shoulder. "I think you guys do pretty well."

"We want to do better. It's better when you're there."

And he needed them.

"What if it doesn't work?"

"What if it does?"

Annie didn't look as if she had any intention of giving up on him, and it struck him that the last thing in the world he would do would be to give up on her.

"Annie...I'm at a disadvantage here."

"I know." She didn't sound one bit displeased. "Bull

riders are stubborn, and I have to take every advantage."

Trace gave a laugh that morphed into a cough that hurt the detached muscles of his sternum.

"I want to come home with you." The hardest words he'd ever said, but once they were out he knew just how true they were. He wanted to go home.

"This seems too easy," Annie said, her gaze narrowed suspiciously.

"No," he said softly. "It's been a while coming. I couldn't stop thinking about you. What I'd given up. My old life didn't seem so good anymore."

He reached out to take her hand, pain shooting through his ribs, but he barely registered it as her fingers entwined with his. "I'm sorry I put you through this," he murmured.

"Yeah, yeah, yeah." But he could see the glimmer of unshed tears in her eyes, and it killed him. "We both had lessons to learn."

"I want out of this bed."

"I want you out of that bed, too. In the worst way." He squeezed her hand. "How are the girls?"

"Resilient. But they miss you."

"I miss them. I worry about them."

Annie smiled softly. "I think that's a pretty universal feeling, in our small universe."

"Annie...I'm not afraid of a half-ton bull, but I'm afraid of failing you." He swallowed hard. "I love you and I left because of that."

For a moment Annie simply stared at him, then she blinked, as if trying to hold back tears. Oh, but he hoped they were happy tears. It would kill him to have hurt her more than he already had. Her grip tightened on his hand and he pulled her closer.

"And now you'll come back for the same reason?" she asked softly.

"If you'll have me."

She wrapped her arms around him and it hurt. He didn't care. He kind of liked the pain because it reminded him that he was alive. "I didn't come all this way because I didn't want you," she murmured before finding his lips, kissing him deeply. "'Cause you know what? I love you, too."

Trace's chest tightened and he brought his hand up to thread through her silky hair, bringing her mouth back down to his and apologizing for everything in the best way he knew how.

Annie sighed against his lips when she finally moved away. "I'm so glad I came. It wasn't an easy decision." She smiled a little. "But I want to make a life with you."

"Do you want me to give up bulls?"

Her eyebrows lifted. "Do I want you to give up breathing?"

He started to smile. She got it. She well and truly got it. And he had her. For his own. He lay back against the stiff hospital pillow, grimacing a little at the deep ache in his side before reaching out to take Annie's hand in his.

Did life get any better than this?

Epilogue

Brick shook his massive head and kicked his back foot, making the metal panel behind him ring.

"You know what?" Trace muttered to the bull, "I feel the same way."

He shot a quick look at the crowd, knew that Annie and the girls were there, somewhere, and that brought on a swell of determination. One, he couldn't get hurt in front of his girls, and two, he was going to take Brick down. The bull hadn't been successfully ridden by anyone in over a year, and it was time.

The bull's muscles bunched as Trace eased himself on, scooting his butt around to find the proper spot to grip with his thighs, push the weight down through his feet before dealing with his rope and glove. The strangest calm settled over him. He usually felt the pump of adrenaline, heard the crowd, but things became oddly silent. The sharp smell of bull sweat still stung his nostrils and he felt the power of the animal between his legs. It was just him and Brick and the contest between them.

Nothing personal, big guy, but I have something to prove.

The gate opened. Brick didn't move, then, just when Trace concluded that his contest was a bust, the bull exploded out into the arena, spinning first left then right. He changed it up with an ass over ears high buck, then started spinning again.

And Trace countered every challenge, his body moving fluidly, despite the jerking, jarring action of the bull beneath him. Oh, yeah, he had this. The buzzer sounded and Trace, for once, disembarked without a face-plant. Only then did he hear the crowd and he raised a hand, pumped his fist. Smiled broadly. Brick continued to buck around the arena until the safety man moved him to the gate, and then the bull trotted out with an until-we-meet-again shake of his horns.

Trace walked to the main gate, feeling…satisfied. Yes, that was the word. He'd be in the money tonight—he was sure of it—but even better, Annie and his girls had been there to witness his triumph.

IT SEEMED LIKE forever before the show ended and Annie was able to herd her excited girls to the area where she was to meet Trace. She saw him instantly, moving a little stiffly as he walked toward them, but she knew that the stiffness came from the previous week's injury. Tonight's ride had been gold.

Kristen and Katie instantly attached themselves to Trace, each taking a hand.

"You were great!" they said in unison. Annie's heart

swelled at Trace's answering smile. He knelt down to look them in the eyes, still holding their hands in his.

"I was aiming for great," he said. "Old Brick isn't very happy with me."

"But we are!" Katie said. "Mom thought we might not want to watch, but I wasn't scared at all!"

Annie had been scared. A little. Common sense scared, but that was part of being involved with a bull rider. They'd been together over six months and it just kept getting better…to the point that when Trace offered her the ring that she'd accidentally come across when he'd asked her to get the tire gauge out of his glove compartment, she knew exactly what her answer was going to be—an unequivocal yes. She'd told him she wouldn't sign up for anything too permanent before a year had passed and he was honoring her wishes.

She was seriously considering pushing the deadline up, especially since Trace was now in partnership with Jasper and working to increase the quality of his bucking stock.

"We can get pizza now, right?" Katie asked.

"Anything you want," Trace said, getting to his feet and pulling Annie into a warm embrace. "Thank you for being here. I couldn't have done it without you."

"There's Lex!" Kristen said, pointing to the walkway leading to the exit.

"You guys can go see her," Annie said. The girls raced off and Annie brought her hands up to frame her bull rider's face, smiling up into his hazel eyes. "I'll just stay here and congratulate the champ."

Her champ leaned down to take her lips and Annie

allowed herself to melt against him until she heard the happy laughter of her daughters.

"Yes," Lex said drily from behind them. "I agree. To-tally mushy."

Trace just smiled and leaned down to kiss her again.

* * * * *

Be sure to check out the first book in Jeannie Watt's
MONTANA BULL RIDERS *series,*
*THE BULL RIDER MEETS HIS MATCH, available
now from Mills & Boon Western Romance. And
look for a new* **MONTANA BULL RIDERS** *story,
coming in 2017!*

MILLS & BOON®

Cherish™

EXPERIENCE THE ULTIMATE RUSH OF FALLING IN LOVE

A sneak peek at next month's titles...

In stores from 8th September 2016:

- **A Mistletoe Kiss with the Boss** – Susan Meier *and*
  Maverick vs Maverick – Shirley Jump
- **A Countess for Christmas** – Christy McKellen *and*
  Ms Bravo and the Boss – Christine Rimmer

In stores from 6th October 2016:

- **Her Festive Baby Bombshell** – Jennifer Faye *and*
  Building the Perfect Daddy – Brenda Harlen
- **The Unexpected Holiday Gift** – Sophie Pembroke *and*
  The Man She Should Have Married – Patricia Kay

Just can't wait?
Buy our books online a month before they hit the shops!
www.millsandboon.co.uk

Also available as eBooks.

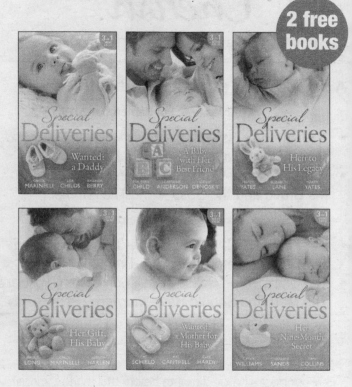